DIAMOND-LAND

LOVING IN MY WORLD IS NEVER EASY

DIAMOND-LAND

LOVING IN MY WORLD IS NEVER EASY

TATIANA

Synopsis

The Zoo Boyz faces a string of misfortunes in the unfolding story, as they try to navigate after Chevy's arrest. As Diamond and the crew fight for Chevy's release, he encounters his own set of issues.

With his grandmother hospitalized, an old flame who cannot let go, and a new love interest, step into his life. The facade he displayed is now being relieved. Upon discovering that his entire childhood has been a lie, Diamond isn't sure how to cope. Questioning who he truly is, he struggles to manage his emotions as he develops feelings for Rayana.

In her efforts to be there for Diamond, Rayana uncovers the unsettling news that her sister is missing. As the two take on each other, challenges arise. As love blossoms in Diamond-Land, chaos takes hold.

Will their love for each other amidst the chaos, and will the Zoo Boyz finally achieve victory?

"Every woman wants the perfect man, even if she falls in love with him in a book."

- Tatiana

Trigga Warnings

Once upon a time in a land so HOOD there live a group of friends where their bad outweighed their good. Using CURSE WORDS is what they understood. From NIGGA to BITCH, and the one thing they don't tolerate is a snitch.

They can be chill, they can be fun, but when people cross them, they'll whip out their GUNS.

Little black boys with deep-rooted TRAUMA, from dealings with wicked girls to their own mommas.

Sometimes they KILL sometimes they FIGHT, but when the sun goes down, they'll FUCK ALL NIGHT.

You may see them coming from afar, but it won't be in a car. Flashing ORANGE lights, not bird, not a plane they'll be on BIKES doing stunts and tricks that's crazily insane.

Brace yourself for a story with LOVE and THRILLS. Please note by the time you get through, you'll be screaming

WE DON'T FUCK YOU, WE ONLY FUCK WITH THE ZOO!

So, before you decide to take a ride, make sure that you have **CLEARED YOUR MIND.**

Tati Thoughts

Sheesh! With each book y'all show out. When this series is over are y'all going to be, ok?

You know how this works if you've been here before THANK YOU! I appreciate all the love I've received for my boys. The way you guys are eating these up is crazy. Thank you for trusting my pen!!

The story will continue as we enter Diamond Land. Please remember these niggas are a brotherhood but they are very different from each other, meaning don't think what you got in Preach story you will get from Diamond. The spice is going to spice when it needs to spice. The drama will be thick, and the audacity will have the nerve.

As you guys continue this series, I hope you're enjoying it but pulling the message behind each story and understand this is about the ZOO BOYZ everything else is extra!

Lastly, there are a few things to remember:

1. Expect the unexpected
2. Enjoy the ride (wear your helmet at all times)
3. The Orange Light Special stays in the book!

Now, Zoo Babies, let's get to the fun shit!
We Only Fuck With The Zoo!

Table of Contents

Playlist

Y'all know we vibe and read over here. Please know you can add the playlist via apple music by following: Freshiebabii

Clouded- Brent Faiyaz - Prologue

Buddy- Musiq Soulchild Pg. 15-21

She'll Be Ok- 4Fargo Pg. 26-28

Loveeeeee Song- Rihanna Ft. Future Pg. 29-32

In My Face- K Camp Pg. 50-54

Love Language- SZA Pg. 55-56

Shake The Room- Pop Smoke Pg. 94-98

Softest Place On Earth- Xscape Pg. 104-110

Make You Mine- Giveon Pg. 111-113

All Mine- Brent Faiyaz Pg. 120-123

More & More- Joe Pg. 131-134

Rodeo(remix)- Lah Pat & Flo Milli Pg. 135-139

Pull Up- LMB DG Pg. 142- 145

Lessons- Eric Roberson Pg.157-163

Fried- Future Pg. 164-167

Streets Made Me A King- Future Pg. 168-173

All To Myself- Unkwnthefaux Pg. 174-175

Try Me- James Brown Pg. 177- 180

All In it- Durty So Clean Pg. 181-184

The Color Orange

Optimism, happiness, enthusiasm, and Connections. As well as displaying creativity, positivity, Transformation, and enlightenment. The color can make people feel outgoing or Bold, and can Strengthen The Emotional Body, encouraging joy, well-being, and cheerfulness. Orange can also project feelings of Arrogance, Pride, impatience, superficiality, and Lack Of Seriousness.

PROLOGUE
DIAMOND

BEFORE ZOO

I laid in bed puffing on some of the best gas I'd ever gotten my hands on. The dark room closed in on me as two bodies swayed back and forth amongst the black light hanging on the wall over my bed frame. Their smiling faces bore into mine. One girl pushed her titties together while the other played with her bare pussy. They both climbed on the bed simultaneously. The cat crawl was sexy as hell.

One beautiful dark skin and the other a peanut butter brown baddie. I spent the day drinking and smoking, trying to suppress everything I was going through. This, however, was the best way to cap off my night. The warm sensation of a tongue gliding up my chest while another pair of lips wrapped around my dick was an indescribable feeling. The smoke lingered from my mouth into the air as I closed my eyes to escape and enjoy my version of paradise.

The sounds of shorty slurping on my dick were like the finest jazz tune. I began humming a melody of my own.

"I want to ride," I heard one of them purr.

"Shit, ride it then," I told her.

I felt her straddle my lap, easing slowly down on top of me. "Mm shit!" I grunted.

The other shorty straddled my face. I sat the blunt down as I munched on her pussy. Her body rocked back and forth. The sounds that filled the room were of a sex escapade worth watching. I tapped the side of shorty ass to get up. "Let's switch this shit up. You on your back and you on your knees."

They both did as I instructed. I stroked brown skin shorty from the back while dark shorty was getting ate. I wanted to forget about my day, my life and everything in between. In a matter of days, my granny was about to lose her house because we couldn't afford to keep up the mortgage. She had used her house as collateral to secure my release because I had been incarcerated a few years ago. I was struggling with life. Nothing was making it better, not even the pussy I fucked on a daily.

I was thinking of my next come-up, the next money grab. Anything I could do to save the house my granny loved and the place I was raised in. That's when the idea of stealing one of the coldest bikes I've seen around came to me. I knew I could get a couple of grand for it and it would buy us some time. I jumped out of the pussy, "Y'all hoes got to go," I said as I grabbed what I needed.

Brown skin shorty popped her head from between the other girl's legs. "Wait, huh?"

I snatched her by her arm. "Get up and get out. Oh, my granny doesn't need to know y'all here so go out of the window."

"Diamond we're not going out the fucking window," she hissed, throwing her hands on her hips.

"If you don't want to get cussed out you gone take your ant-shaped ass out that window."

Both girls smacked their lips as they got dressed. I honestly didn't care because I was on a mission. Pussy came and went like a thief in the night. By tomorrow, I'll have two different bitches in here. Once they were gone. I threw on my black hoodie and sweats before leaving my room.

As I reached the front door, the sound of my granny made me stop, "Listen here Chew, it's later than the devil's hoe den out there. Whatever it is you think you're about to get into you better think twice," she said as she came up behind me, placing her hand on mine. My granny had always been so protective over me. I never understood what her reasons for keeping me so close were, but it was as if she was shielding me from the world. Sometimes I'd felt so sheltered, but grateful she had taken me in.

"I rather you be back there with those no manners having hussies than out in those streets Chew Chew," she pleaded.

I hated when she called me that. Every time she said it, I backed off whatever I was doing, but tonight she would have to forgive me because there was no way in hell, I was letting her lose this house. I said nothing. I kissed her on her forehead, before leaving.

I tossed my hood on my head as I made my way down the street. The night air had the demon wrapped in it, but tonight, he and I would have to go head-to-head over my granny. She was my life, all I knew. To me, I didn't have parents; she was that. I was in a place in my life where nothing mattered but her.

My entire walk, I thought of my granny being put out of the placed she was most comfortable, and it made me sick. I felt less than a man. My grandma was taking care of me, and I couldn't do anything to pour back into her. I felt helpless. I promised myself I was done with this shit, but I felt like I had no other option. A nigga couldn't get a regular job because of my record, and I was no street hustler. I was simply a nigga who was good at stealing cars and beating niggas asses.

I remembered my first time. Granny was sick and her insurance wouldn't cover her medicine. So, I snuck out one night and went a few blocks over. I popped the lock on a clean-ass Benz, wired it up, and took off. After that, shit was like a cakewalk until; I got caught. I did a short bid, and now here I was about to do the shit all over again for my granny. I strolled through the streets until I reached my destination.

I heard there was a new crew of bikers that had just started doing street races, but the underground street world didn't take them seriously. They were easy targets. Nobody was checking for them. I crept up on the side of the hall where two bikes sat outside, but the one I was looking for had a shiny orange tail. When I spotted it, I rubbed my hands together.

I was good at stealing cars, but bikes were different. I'm sure the wiring was about the same. I made my way up to the bike which sat below a window. I peered inside to see two niggas sitting there talking. On the table was a gun. I needed to be quick and smart. I pulled out my tool, eased on the bike, pulled the wires, cut them, and put the two I needed together. I started that bitch up, revved it, hopped on, and took off.

Bloaw!

The bullet whistled past my head, but I kept going. "This is for you granny," I said to myself.

I rode that bitch through the city like the fucking nightrider until I reached Rock's garage. Rock was the king of the projects who owned a chop shop. When his people let me in, the sounds of his team working on cars, breaking them down, and shaving numbers off consumed the warehouse. Rock came up to me. "Fuck is this? What am I supposed to do with a fucking bike?" he turned to his people and laughed.

I scratched the back of my head. "Nigga sell it, I don't know. This is a Premium fucking bike. Look at spoilers. The paint job. The fucking engine," I tried to explain.

Rock surveyed the bike. "What you want for it?"

"Shit, these normally go for like thirty grand considering the paint job and all the extras on—"

He laughed loudly, "Nigga this ain't no dealership, ten bands."

Ten thousand was barely enough to do what I needed to. "I was thinking twenty."

Rock stepped closer to me. He went to say something until the sounds of bullets penetrating the garage doors caused havoc in the warehouse.

"Nigga you set me up!" Rock gritted.

I dropped to the ground, trying to crawl my ass up out of there. When they kicked the door down. The two niggas I stole the bike from came in airing that bitch out. The same niggas that were supposed to be Rock's soldiers were dropping like flies or running. I'd finally made it to the back door. I needed to get back to my granny. What I didn't want was her crying over my body.

Bloaw! Bloaw!

The first bullet went over my head hitting the top of the door, the other hit my arm. "Shit!"

I turned to see Rock coming up behind me, aiming his gun. "I don't like to be played for a fool. Shit was cool until your pretty boy-looking ass came in here trying to hustle me."

I held onto my arm. The only person I could think about was my granny. How she warned me. How I had failed her so many times and this was another thing added to the long list of shit I had put her through. There was no way I wasn't making it back to her tonight. I rushed Rock, knocking the gun out of his hand. I was on fight or flight.

Whap! Whap!

I pounded on Rock so bad his body bounced off the concrete. Rock shifted his body, kicking me backward into the door. He picked up his gun coming up to me holding the gun to my head, "I'm sorry Granny," was all I could say.

"You got two seconds to get that shit off him or niggas gone be smoking yo ass, like a rock," A guy I had never seen before gritted.

Rock slowly turned around, "Fuck, is you? Super nigga?"

"Nah, I'm from the fuckin Zoo, nigga!"

I rushed up to Rock snatched the gun out of his hand and was now aiming it at the front of his forehead. I glanced at the other guy behind him. Nigga was on demon time. His demeanor displayed one of a king. One who didn't give a shit about nothing; not even death. He glanced at me then back at

Rock. I went to pull the trigger on Rock, but he shot before I could.

Bloaw!

He sent one through Rock's head with the bullet missing me by an inch. He came up to me. "You like stealing shit huh?"

Shit, nigga they about to open my top like a soup can. "I heard about you Diamond Blanco. You ride?"

I nodded.

"What the fuck you stealing for, you a broke nigga?"

The other guy came walking up. That's when I realized he was the nigga that lived up the block from my granny. I dropped my head.

"Sup Diamond," he chimed in.

"Man, fuck! Look, I-I was trying to help my granny."

"You a dumb nigga, but I get it. We want you to ride with us," the demon-looking nigga said to me.

Hell, if it spared me death, I was on board. I followed them back to the hall. They made me ride the bike I stole. When I went into the building, he sat the gun on the table. "This nigga right there is Zu," he pointed to the nigga that stayed on my granny's block.

I saw him here and there, but my focus was never on the niggas, only the women. They praised me like I was some sort of celebrity, and I fed into it every time.

He then pointed to another nigga sitting at the table putting together a gun. "I'm Foe."

The demon-looking nigga walked to the back, returning with a duffle bag in his hand, tossing it to me.

"I get it you a young nigga, probably get pussy every day, but out here fighting demons. I'm going to take care of you. Show you some shit, but I want you to ride. You're a fast little nigga and we can use you," he said to me. "Look at me when I'm talking to you. When you are speaking man to man you look them in their eyes!" he snapped.

I looked at him. There was no fear in his eyes this nigga was on pure king status.

"You should have been the one with the smoke signal coming from your temple, but you're here," he said to me.

When I opened the bag, all I saw was stacks of money. "That should be enough to take care of your granny and get yo own spot. Don't be in her shit causing havoc. You're grown get your own. Get your shit in order."

I glanced at both the other guys. Zu pointed to him. "That's Chevy."

"But I can't pay you back."

Chevy came closer to me, "First thing I need you to do is listen. You don't have to pay me back, but you do have to ride. Can you do that?"

Zu laughed. "The green-eyed bandit is nice on the bike. Little nigga got hands too."

Chevy crossed his arms over his chest. "What's it going to be?"

Foe slammed his hand on the table. "This is a brotherhood. We got your back."

I glanced at the money, then at them. It almost felt like a movie the way they saved me. Rock was going to kill me either way. I saw it in his eyes. Maybe this is where God was leading me tonight.

"I'll ride," I mumbled.

Zu tossed me a helmet while Chevy pointed to the bike I stole. "That shit is yours."

They said in unison.

"Welcome to the muhfuckin Zoo!"

DIAMOND- LAND

DIAMOND- LAND

DIAMOND- LAND

DIAMOND LAND

GREEN- EYE BANDIT
Facade has taken a toll on Diamond as he can no longer hide when he finds out the truth about the life he once knew.

THE ZOO
Where all the dirty work takes place

ORANGE VILLAGE
Where the parties and discussions are had. The Boyz safe space.

PENTHOUSE
Where Ravana is fully introduced to Diamond's sexual world.

DIAMOND'S LOUNGE
Diamond's place of solace

DIAMOND-LAND
Where he finds the true meaning of Diamond-Land

Seeing Preach in the pulpit doing his thing made me feel like a proud big brother. He stood up there, conquering his fears. However, we had a problem. Chevy was being arrested. They walked him out of the church, and we all rushed behind him. "Chev, we got you. We're going to get you out!" I shouted.

Foe ran up to the detective's side, stopping him from walking further. "Fucking pig nigga!" he growled at him.

Foe didn't care that we had just come out of the church. Zu was on the other side. "He ain't do shit, yo Chev, my nigga we are getting you out."

2

I could see Preach running out, still in the robe. "Chevy!" he shouted.

Chevy's head slowly turned. "We got you. Zoo over everything," he said.

Chevy glanced at all of us, then Harvey. "Get her out of here," he grumbled.

Harvey's wails made us look at her. Zu wrapped her in his arms, then picked her up, taking her to his ride. I ran my hands over my head. This was an added stress to my life. I still hadn't gotten over the fact that God was trying to take my granny early. I knew she couldn't be here forever, but I was selfish and I wanted her to stay longer. I prayed so hard that he would give me more time. So far, he's been listening.

Granny is in the hospital recovering, but as long as she was breathing, I would walk to that muhfucka every day if I had to.

Now one of my best friends was being locked up. It seemed like as soon as everything was going well for the crew; we got pushed ten steps back somehow. We'd all decided to go up to the precinct to get him out. I rode with Foe to church, but I didn't want to leave Chevy's Caprice sitting out here.

"Aye Foe, I'm taking the Caprice."

"Bet."

It wasn't like I needed keys because I knew how to steal cars. It was a part of my past. It was like riding a fucking bike. The key was not to fuck up his car, otherwise, when he got out, he would rip my braids right out of my head. I jogged across the street to his ride.

"Diamond!" someone called out.

I turned to look, and it was Rayana. Her pretty chocolate face held worry in her eyes. It had always been something about a dark-brown-skinned girl that made a nigga's knees weak. Her full lips, big brown eyes, and slim frame were perfect. Since my birthday she and I talked here and there but it had been nothing serious. I wanted to ask her out but right now wasn't the time.

"Is everything ok?" she asked.

"Always."

The thing had always been to tell people we were always alright even if we weren't. Chevy always said never let a nigga see you sweat, and we stuck beside those words.

She started to say something else, but her pops called out to her, "Ray, let's go!" he yelled.

It was something about his ass that seemed off. Preach told us how the nigga didn't like him. If he didn't like Preach, he would for sure not like me. Rayana stood there as her eyes bounced between me and her pops. As much as a nigga wanted to chit-chat, I needed to leave.

Once inside the car, I went to work snatching the wires down, placing the ones I needed together to start it up, putting the car in gear. I glanced out the window with Rayana gazing at me as I took off.

My nerves were fucked up. As soon as I passed the church, I let loose. *Fuck! Shit! Fuck. Fuck, Fuck!*

I joked around a lot because it was how I coped with my stress. Today, however, all my stress was catching up to me. I was finding it harder to keep my shit together. It took me no time to get to the precinct. Zu, Foe, and Harvey were waiting outside. I got out of the car walking up to them. "Why is she here?" I asked.

"Nigga because that's my friend too. I want to be here!" Harvey snapped.

I knew Chevy didn't want her around, but shit, she was a part of everything else. My eyes landed on Zu. He should have taken her ass home, but the way his nose was open for Harvey, she probably convinced the nigga to bring her here. Before going inside, the sound of Preach yelling caught our attention.

"So y'all was about to go in there without me?"

Foe shrugged. "Shit, I figured you was staying back at church. You looked good up there boy," he laughed.

"Thank you. Let's go get our brother out," he said as we all walked into the building together.

All eyes were on us as we stepped inside. Me being here brought back so many memories, ones I tried forgetting.

Preach walked over to the front desk. "We're here to place bail for June Calloway."

The clerk eyes raised to him. "Do you know how much his bail is?"

Preach smiled. "I didn't ask you how much, I said we want to bail him out."

She placed her eyes back on the screen and pecked at the keyboard.

"Any slower the nigga gone be hauled off somewhere," Zu jumped in.

"He has no bail," she smirked, and so did Preach.

He glanced back at us, then at her. "Then we're not going no fucking where."

She glanced back down at the screen, then at all of us again. "He needs to go before a judge to determine if he will get bail and if so, how much."

Preach pushed his glasses up. "Ma'am, I just came from church today giving thanks to God and prayed that he would keep me sane. However, all this extra shit you talking, you will need the prayer more than me if you don't—"

The door swung open to Navi coming in. She glanced at Preach, who took a quick look at her, then back at the front desk worker.

"Detective Richardson!" the front desk worker said in relief.

"Detective?" we all said but Preach.

Harvey turned to him. "So, you been fucking a pig?"

Preach rolled his head in a circle. I couldn't believe it.

Harvey shot up from the chair, rushing over to Navi, "You snake ass bitch!"

Another officer came from the back and Zu and Foe stood.

"We won't be doing none of that," Zu said.

"We're ok," Navi told the officer.

Harvey was ready to open a can of whoop ass and frankly, her being a cop, I would have sat back and watched. Navi didn't care about Harvey at all, though. The only person she cared to get a response from was the one nigga who stood there ignoring her, Preach. I guess she realized the nigga wasn't about to talk to her, so she made her way to the back.

Hours had passed by before someone came out, only to tell us they wouldn't release him until he saw a judge. We'd all headed out of the building. I knew the city wouldn't sleep as long as Chevy was locked up. We agreed to wait until court before causing havoc. As much as I wanted to stay around, I still needed to go see my granny.

I showed Harvey how to start Chevy's caprice so she could take it to the house. While Foe agreed to take me home to grab my car. We all dapped each other up as we took off. I was concerned about Chevy, but right now I needed to make sure my granny was going to be straight.

I opened my eyes to the sounds of gurgling. My eyes scanned around as they landed on someone throwing up in the trash. The cold room I was in smelled like a locker room full of dirty men. The smell was so strong it made my stomach curl. I sat in a corner with my hands tied behind my back. With everything going on in my life this had to happen to me.

The universe wasn't playing fair. I knew I should have stayed my ass on that bus, but it was something that led me to my store. An energy drew me there, but I wasn't expecting this. The boy had now stood wiping his mouth with the back of his hand.

"You shouldn't kidnap people on an empty stomach," I said to him.

"Shut up!" he spat.

"Ginger helps. Get you some tea, add some ginger and you will feel better."

He glared at me like I was the evil person. I was simply trying to help him. He was young, no older than eighteen or nineteen. I could tell he'd never done anything like this before because guilt settled on his face. As he paced the room I tried fiddling with the cord around my wrists. I was getting the fuck out of here. A part of me regretted turning my location off and disposing of my phone. If I couldn't get out of here, I prayed my family would realize I was missing and come looking for me. Hell, Navi was a detective she did shit like this all the time. Me and my sisters weren't as close as we should have been. I felt like my parents catered to them like they were the only two who mattered so I distanced myself from all of them. Now, I wish I hadn't.

My eyes landed back on the young boy whose face was now flushed. I was almost certain he was the weakest link; a good conversation and some guilt trip thrown in there would break him.

"It's fucking hot," he mumbled.

"I mean you can open a window or two. Listen, I'm going to be honest if you don't let me go, you will die," I rambled.

9

"Why don't you just shut up."

I shrugged my shoulders, "You guys took me. Hell, it's better than being stuck in my house with a damn ankle monitor on though."

I was trying my best to play it cool. However, deep down inside I was fucking scared. The thought of me not making it out of here terrified me. I knew all of this had to do with Cortez. I saw all the red flags hanging over his head and his dick and I ignored them; now here I was. I hated Cortez and if I could kill him, I would. The sound of a door opening startled me.

"Listen up!" someone yelled.

When he stepped into my view it was the same guy that came into my store looking for Cortez. Then more of Blaze N Fire appeared. *Shit, it's a lot of them.* One of them I recognized. *Malik?* I couldn't believe this. The guy began talking, "I did my homework on those Zoo Boyz. One of those niggas is responsible for killing my brother Rock. So not only did I lose money giving it to this bitch," he pointed at me, "I find out that one of those muscle head niggas killed my brother. I want them nigga's heads."

"So, you take me because of some niggas I don't know!" I snapped.

He turned to me smiling. "Lucas, man I've been trying to get her to shut up," the young boy said to him.

"I lost out on a hundred bands," he paused now stooping down in front of me. "It has everything to do with you, mama. Cortez owes a lot of money and you're his collateral. Oh, and that super nigga that called himself saving you, his ass got to go too," he said rubbing my cheek.

"Fuck you! I have nothing to do with Cortez."

He ignored me turning back toward his crew. Malik came forward, "One of them live right across from me."

I jumped in because if he thought I was giving him that money I wasn't. "I'm not giving you shit. Your best bet would be to let me go. What you should have done is worried less about the Zoo Boyz and more about me. You have no idea who you kidnapped!"

My shit talking was beginning to get to him. He held his hand out as someone handed him tape. "Nobody wants to hear this bitch rambling," he grumbled.

They gave him tape and just like that he placed the tape across my mouth now, focusing his attention back on his crew. A tear escaped me this time because I wanted to get out of here. I was feeling defeated. As much as I needed a savior, I was praying Mystery Man found me somehow as he had done before.

I finally reached the hospital making my way to my grandmother's room. As soon as I stepped inside, she turned to look at me.

"Granny, you're up," I said happy to see she was now awake.

The last couple of days she has been out of it. They told me that with her being unconscious for as long as she was some of her memory and motor skills had diminished. She hadn't talked since being here. Chevy and I made sure she had not only the best care but the best doctors to try to get her back to her normal self. Although, I was in the streets I was still a praying man and made sure to pray over her every night.

I noticed someone leaned over on the side of her when they lifted, I snapped. "Fuck is you doing here Mo?"

She stood. "Diamond I was checking on her."

I dropped my head. "Nigga fuck you good and now you in here trying to play nurse Betty with my granny?"

Monette being here without permission pissed me off. I knew before leaving here today, I was going to change all of that. Seeing her repeatedly made me question if she was worth giving another chance, but right now I didn't want her here.

She stood there gazing at me as if she was trying to speak with her eyes. I snapped my finger "Earth to Mo, get out," I gritted. "I got ninety-nine problems and Mo you the main one," I snapped.

"Diamond why are you treating me like this? You're not the same guy that I met. I'm not a bad person," she tried explaining.

I knew she wasn't a bad person, but she betrayed me. I felt like I had given her plenty of opportunities to come clean and she didn't. I don't think she understands the situation she'd put me in. What she did could have cost not only me my life, but my brothers. If she needed protection she should have said it, but she said nothing but a bunch of moaning when we fucked.

I really wasn't a relationship type nigga, anyways. I've dated a lot of women but none of them had been worth keeping, Mo included. I swiftly moved toward her placing my fingers to her chin, "You're not a bad person Mo," I said, bringing my face closer to hers. "You're just not my person."

I'm sure my words cut her deep, but I wanted her to understand there was nothing between us, but sex. The shit was great, but nothing worth fighting for. I did however appreciate her persistence. Mo was faced with death in that warehouse and still she wanted a nigga. She went to touch my face when I heard someone enter the room.

"Sorry, I—"

When I glanced back it was Yana. I quickly moved away from Mo. Yana glanced at both of us. Mo took one last look at me before leaving the room making sure to brush past Yana. Something told me this wouldn't be the end of Mo. I wasn't sure what it was going to take for her to understand I just hope like hell I didn't have to put her down like Zu did Triece.

I'd just arrived at work and clocked in. I loved my job, but it was taking a toll on me. It was a lot to handle between the double shifts and studying to become a registered nurse. Despite the busyness of my life, I showed my family a different side. For a while, I figured my sisters were living their best lives only to find out they had been faking just as I have.

As I prepared to check on my patients, I thought about Diamond. I wanted to tell Diamond so badly about what I knew about Chevy, but it wasn't my place. Seeing them all worried about him, I just didn't want to give them more news I knew they couldn't handle.

Chevy reminded me much of Zari. They were both bullheaded and guarded. The same fear his face held when he found out I knew about what he was keeping from his friends was the same look of fear Zari had when she lied to my parents about her being a therapist. She thought I didn't know, but I did. Me and my sister used to be close, but something happened where we had lost our closeness. I didn't know if it was that we'd become too busy for each other or Zari feeling like we really didn't accept her for her. She had always felt like Daddy was picking sides and my mom didn't see things her way. Every time Navi and I tried talking to her about it, she would shut us out, so I simply stopped reaching out.

I'd just stepped into Diamond's grandmother's room. I didn't request her; they placed Gloria on the floor I worked on. It was nice getting to know her, though. She didn't talk to the other nurses, only me, which was cool. It surprised me to see not only Diamond in the room, but the girl I had gotten into a fight with on his birthday. She looked so familiar, but I couldn't put my finger on where I knew her from. I could tell there were feelings there because of the way she looked at him. She was in love with this man. The question was, did he feel the same way, because the nigga that was grinding all on me at the party didn't seem like a man in love.

Diamond and I weren't a thing, but he and I had been talking here and there. After his birthday party, I didn't want to have nothing to do with him. The one thing I prided myself on was not fighting over a man. I could tell by how he moved he had a plethora of women flocking after him and I wasn't going to be one of them.

Navi was head over heels for his friend Preach. Zari was finally getting over Cortez. However, her hard head made a soft ass. Navi told me she had gotten arrested after trying to call herself breaking into that broke nigga's house. I refused to be one of those women. My sisters did enough of the crazy shit for me. I had been meaning to call and check on Zari since being put on house arrest, but I was so busy I barely had time for myself.

I hesitated stepping further inside the room because I was torn between giving them time to talk or focusing on my job. Before I could decide, she abruptly left the room, purposefully brushing her shoulder against mine. I dropped my head, biting into my lip because what I wanted to do was snatch her by her hair, trying to rip the lace off her fucking head.

Diamond walked to the other side of the bed, holding his grandma's hand. "You're her nurse?" he asked.

"You see me here don't you," I rolled my eyes.

"Damn why you got an attitude?"

I said nothing as I checked Gloria's vitals, giving her all my attention. "Hey Gloria, how are you feeling?"

Diamond leaned his head forward to get me to look at him. "She can't talk."

Still ignoring him, I continued. "Gloria, girl, I went to church today service was so good." I smiled.

"Damn, you got a pretty smile."

I cut my eyes at him. "Diamond, please. If you're not going to help me care for her, please leave the room until I'm finished," I hissed.

He came around to the side I was on, standing so close I could smell his cologne. The nigga smelled amazing.

"Why you acting stank? Your mad cause she was in here, listen baby—"

I threw my hand up, cutting him off. "First, I don't care what you two were in here talking about. Second, I'm not chasing no nigga. So, if you're worried about me being pressed, I'm not."

He held both his hands up, backing away. I continued to help his grandma as he sat back and watched.

"And she can talk by the way," I mumbled.

"How you know?" he snapped.

I giggled. "Oh, so now you have an attitude. Go figure."

18

He crossed his arms over his chest, "You pretty and all but you have a smart-ass mouth."

"And?"

"And I got something that can fix that."

"What?"

"This dick!" he spat.

"Chew, Chew!" Gloria said, now looking at him.

He looked at her, then at me. "I told you." I shrugged.

He rushed back to her side, taking her hand into his. "Sorry Granny," he said, kissing the side of her face. "It's her fault. She made a nigga slip up."

I could tell he adored her. It let me know he had a sensitive side, and it was cute. However, that pretty boy player shit was tired.

"Let me take you out," I heard him say.

I rolled the sheets on top of Gloria as I finished up. I went to head out of the room, but stopped to give Diamond's fine ass one last look. "No," I said as I exited the room.

If Diamond wanted me, he was going to have to work way harder than that. Besides, I needed to make sure whatever him and ole girl had was dead because what I didn't need was to catch a case over him and I was still dealing with someone.

***

I finally finished my shift. The day had taken a toll on me, and I wanted to dive right into my bed. As I exited the hospital heading to my car, a pair of lights flashed in my face, causing me to throw my hand over my forehead, trying to shield my eyes from the brightness. I stuck my other hand in my purse for my mase because if I had to; I wasn't going down without a fight. The lights suddenly shut off, allowing me to get a better look.

The first thing I spotted was a bouquet of orange fully bloomed hydrangeas. When they lowered, his face appeared.

He started singing, and it sounded so good. *"Pardon, darling, if I alarmed ya, I don't mean to bother ya, I just wanna, get you to pause and slow ya walk."*

A giggle escaped my lips.

"Since you had an attitude earlier, I figured these would make you smile," Diamond said as he came up to me, handing me the flowers.

I swear I didn't want to, but I couldn't help it. I smiled hard. "That's what I'm talking about a pretty ass smile for a pretty ass woman."

I continued to make my way to my car with him right on my heels. "Damn, you going to let a nigga take you out or what?"

I stopped walking, turning to give him my attention. "No," I said to him. "Flowers are nice, the singing is a plus, but they don't impress me. I can promise you Diamond, I'm not like any other woman you had before, try harder, or don't try at all," I told him.

He put his hands behind his back, coming into my space. Diamond was so close I could feel his breath on my forehead. Leaning down, he winked, "Yana, I always get what I want. You trying to make me beg and I'm not doing that. We will see who taps out first," he said, smiling, backing away, and walking to his car.

He must have thought I was playing when I said he needed to try harder. If he wanted me to be around, I had to know he wanted just me and not anyone else.

CHAPTER TWO

PREACH

Applying Pressure

I sat in the dark living room, allowing my thoughts to consume me. There were so many questions I had, not for God, but for Pretty. Shit happened so fast today that I didn't have time to bask in my sermon. *First thought*, did Chevy now look at me differently? *Second thought*, how could Pretty not know what her father was doing? I leaned back on the couch, resting my head. I heard the locks click, then the lights snapped on.

"Preach!" Navi shouted. "How the hell you get in here?"

"I can do anything through Christ who strengthens me, and he gave me the strength to break in yo shit," I gritted. "See, how fast I can switch up? One minute I'm preaching and praising the lord. The next minute I'm the hood nigga you never asked for. Get over here and sit the fuck down."

My words surprised Pretty because I had never been so aggressive towards her since the first day we met. However, I was mad and hurt. I felt betrayed. She scooted her feet over toward me, sitting in the chair. I placed prayer hands to my lips. "I asked you if you were still on the case and you told me no. You lied."

Pretty leaned forward, placing her hand to mine. "Preach I fucking swear I said nothing. It was my father. I love you; I wouldn't betray you like that," she tried explaining.

I shot up from the couch, "Are you still on the fucking case or not?"

"I am."

I clapped my hands together. *"Fuck!"*

I love Pretty. She means a lot to me, but the love I have for Chevy was one she couldn't replace and if I had to choose, it would be him over her. He was solid he never switched up. The nigga would give his life for any of us, and we couldn't do right by him. She stood up, trying to touch me, but I didn't want to be touched.

"Preach, I still have a job to do. Whether it's on this case or not I'm still a cop. You knew this before you kissed me for the first time, hell before you finger fucked me on the rooftop, you knew. So, what do you want me to do? Quit? Because I can't. Just how you're trying to protect your friend I'm trying to protect my sister," she explained.

I didn't know what I wanted her to do. I could take care of Pretty. It wasn't a problem, but I also didn't want her to have to choose. That was something I dealt with for so long I knew how it felt. I didn't know where she and I would go from here, because the next thing I was about to tell her was going to fuck her head up.

She took my hand into hers. "If you want this shit to disappear y'all need to figure out what happened the night he murdered his father. I will try and do as much as I can on my end. Baby, we're a team."

I nodded slowly. "Remember when I told you there would be a time you will need God and you better learn to pray, well the time is now. Your father, Daddy fucking dearest that nigga is dead," I stroked her face. "He's only doing this to get to me. See, Pretty what he doesn't know is he found the right nigga on the wrong fucking day. At this point, I don't even think prayer is going to work. The nigga he locked up is like a father to me and if you think for a single fucking minute I'm going to sit back and do nothing, Pretty, you will learn today."

She searched my eyes. "What are you saying to me? You're trying to kill my father?"

"No, baby, I'm not trying, I am. Do with that what you will," I finished, kissing her forehead, before leaving her house.

I prayed she could forgive a nigga for what was to come. I meant what I said. I just hoped she could understand and her love for me was strong enough to stay around. As bad as I wanted to let her go, I couldn't because I was in love.

I pulled into the parking garage to my crib. Before getting out, I took a deep breath. Today has been a lot. From Chevy being arrested to Mo showing up at the hospital playing nurse Betty with my granny. It was all draining. I got out, jumping on the elevator then straight into my crib. Normally, when I came in, I would roll a blunt, smoke, then shower the day away. Tonight, would be the opposite.

I got in the shower almost immediately after walking into my place. I could hear my phone vibrating, but I tried ignoring it. The more it went off, I became worried. *What if it was about my granny?* I quickly cut the shower off before getting out. When I glanced at the phone, it was a bunch of missed calls from Mo. Then a message came in that she was at my door. I wrapped a towel around my waist, rushing out of the bathroom, storming to my front door. I swung it open, "Fuck do you want? And why you blowing up my phone like you're dying?"

She said nothing. She opened her coat, exposing her naked body. I dropped my head. "Come on Mo, let's not do this."

"I'm standing here in front of you ready and you're going to turn me down?"

I couldn't lie. Mo was looking good as hell. I hadn't touched her since the night at the lounge when I found out about her fucking lies. I pinched the bridge of my nose, then slowly raised my eyes to her. *Fuck!* This was part of my problem not turning down good pussy. I knew the thought shouldn't have crossed my mind, but it did. I snatched her by her waist, pulling her inside, closing the door behind her.

I placed my lips to her collarbone, letting my tongue stroke her a few times. I could hear her hissing as I eased the coat off her. I place my hand to the back of her neck, spinning her and slamming her body against the door.

"Don't fucking move. You want dick and I'm going to give you just that," I whispered in her ear.

I walked to the back to grab a condom. There was no way I was fucking her raw again. I didn't need any babies with her

27

ass. Crazy thing is, I actually like Mo, but what she did, I didn't know if I could ever trust her and for me, that was a problem. I strolled back into the living room, and she was still standing there, facing the door. She wanted this dick bad. I removed the towel, sliding the condom on. I tossed my hair in a bun because I didn't want her pulling on my shit. I crept up behind her, caressing the side of her body. The way Mo trembled, I knew it wouldn't take her long to cum. I moved her hair to the side as my free hand gripped my dick, sliding up and down her ass.

"Mo, I thought the dick I served you last time was enough to hold you over, but I see it wasn't so let's try this again."

"Sssss," she hissed. "Diamond I—"

"Aht, ah, Mo you know the rules no talking. Unless I'm filling that pretty fucking mouth with dick I don't want to hear it."

She rolled her head in a full circle, planting her forehead to the door. I entered her warm center slow. "Mm, shit!" I grunted.

"*Ah*," she whined.

I knew all of this was wrong. Monette had great pussy, and I hated she betrayed me. The more I began thinking about it, the more my hips moved with anger. I went from gripping her waist to taking a handful of her hair into my hand, bringing her head back slightly pressing my chest against her back.

Her panting became loud. "Fuck Diamond!" she screamed. "That's right fuck Diamond, remember that when I'm done. This shit can't happen again, fuck this feels so good," I growled.

My slow strokes turned into hard thrusts. I was sending Mo's body up and down like a fucking sling shot.

"Why does this feel so good? Don't stop, please," she cried.

"It's got to stop. Next time you show up unannounced Mo, I will shoot you."

She pushed her ass out, swiveling her hips. She tried slowing down my pace to control my movements, but I fixed that quick. *One hand to the back of her neck, the other to her waist.* I moved her to the back of the couch as I used one leg to pry hers open and placed my other leg on the back of the couch.

She tried moving from my grasp, but my grip on her was too tight. "Nah, no running. Take all this hood dick!" I barked.

"I love you Diamond," she moaned.

I stopped. "What you just say?"

Her head turned toward me nervously, "I-I said I love you," she stuttered.

I knew what I had done was a bad idea and instantly regretted it. I liked Mo, yes, but love her no. I tried the relationship shit before. I gave my heart to a woman who told me all I was good for was being eye candy and fucking.

Honestly, she was right. I had nothing to offer her but dick at the time. What I couldn't understand was if she loved me, why couldn't we figure it out? A nigga was down, and I needed someone other than my granny, but I had no one but myself until I became part of Zoo. I just promised myself this heart of mine was staying where it was and wasn't being handed out like a piece of fucking candy.

I pulled out, "You got to go, Mo," I told her calmly.

She stood straight up, trying to gaze into my eyes. I pulled my eyes away from her. "Monette, I don't love you. If I say I do, it would be only to please you in the moment. This cannot happen again and that's the nicest way I can put it."

Her eyes bounced all over the place, but she didn't move. I clapped my hands making her jump. "Mo!"

"Diamond, I don't understand. I know I messed up but we're all human. I'm trying to show you I'm not who you think I am," she tried explaining.

The entire situation was fucked up. *Could I give her another chance?* She wanted to try again. Then I thought about Yana. When I saw her for the first time, it was like an instant connection. It was something about her not falling for the simple shit I liked. Yana did, however, want a nigga to chase her and I couldn't see myself doing that, but the feeling of not knowing what being with her would be like came to mind. I was becoming confused, and I didn't like the feeling.

Monette stepped in front of me, placing both hands to my face, forcing me to look at her. "It's something here Diamond, I know it is. I will back away, but I want to show you I'm not who you think I am," she whispered.

She removed her hands from my face, and walked back over to her coat, picking it up and sliding it on. I removed the condom, threw it in the trash, grabbed my towel and wrapped it back around my waist. The silence between us was awkward. I'd never in my life stop fucking because of words, but this situation was different. Mo was lonely. She needed someone to fill a void, one that I couldn't fill. The type of love she needed wasn't from a man, but from her family. I opened the door for her, allowing her to walk out when my eyes landed on Rayana. She was coming up the hall with her head down, engrossed in her phone. When she lifted her head, she looked at Mo, then at me. *Shit!*

"I knew you looked familiar," she said to Mo.

What the fuck was she talking about? Monette didn't respond as she kept walking until she was in the elevator. Rayana continued to walk until she reached the door across from me. *She was fucking with the nigga, Malik.* She still hadn't said a word to me. Instead, she acted as if I didn't exist, and it bothered me.

"So, you're going to ignore me?" I asked her.

I felt played. I had never seen her here before, or was it I had never paid attention? I didn't know if this was a sign that me making Monette leave was the right choice, but I was going to take advantage.

She turned her head glancing at me. The smile that appeared on her face was one of *fuck you*. I knew Mo had just left, which didn't make the situation better. Rayana and I weren't even on that level, but something about knowing she was going to walk through that nigga's door and get her cheeks clapped bothered me. She knocked on his door while I stood there watching like a fucking sucker. I heard his locks click, and I did the only thing I felt was right. I snatched her ass, pulled her into my crib, and closed the door.

I had been sitting on this hard ass floor for hours. My legs were going numb, my head was hurting, and I had to pee. I glanced up at the young boy. It was clear they made him the babysitter. "Hey!" I called out.

He slowly raised only his eyes to me.

"I got to pee," I whined.

"So."

"So, nigga you want me to piss on your floor? The least thing you can do is show me the bathroom," I said to him.

I had a plan. As soon as he let me go to the bathroom, I was hauling ass. I just needed to survey the area first and I was gone. "What's your name?" I asked trying to have some type of small talk.

"What do you care? You need to be worried about what Lucas is going to do with you if Cortez ass doesn't show up."

If they were waiting on Cortez, I was for sure dead. He was a coward, a broke nigga who stole my money and placed me in this situation. If my life was in the hands of Cortez, I was not going to make it out of here alive which further made me start panicking. My breathing began to pick up because my nerves were getting the best of me. I shook my head to rid the nerves, but they wouldn't let up.

Breathe in, breathe out. Breathe in, breathe out.

My small breaths turned into loud pants. I was losing it. "I have to fucking pee!" I screamed.

He stood from the chair, coming over to me. "Calm the fuck down," he grumbled.

Calm down? I was dying, whether by them or myself, from panicking. He held a grip on my arm, lifting me up. He reached under the cabinet, grabbed a bucket, and slid it in front of me. "What the fuck is that?"

"You said you had to piss, so you going to piss in this bucket."

I needed a bathroom and a window to climb out of. I needed to fucking run. I glanced at him as he held no sympathy in his face. "Look, it's either me or you, and I damn sure don't want to be on anyone's headstone." He shrugged. "And you think I want to? I have a family that I'm sure is looking for me. Listen, boy!"

"The name is Ace."

"Well, Ace," I paused. "I need to pee, and I'm not using that."

"Shit, then you gone piss on yourself," he said, heading back toward the chair.

"Ok!"

He stopped, turned, and came back toward me. "I'm going to undo your hands. If you try something, I will shoot you."

I nodded. The relief my arms felt was incredible. He stood there watching. "Turn around," I mumbled.

"No!"

"Fine."

I pulled my pants down and pissed in the bucket. He pulled his eyes away, and then they landed back on me. "Tissue?"

He handed me a crumbled-up paper towel. When I was done, I stood there. "You know Malik is going to get you guys killed. I know him. He's an idiot and one my sister should have left alone."

"I don't give a fuck. I won't be here long anyway."

35

I could tell he was a lost soul, one that was only around because he had to be. The energy he gave was scared. A façade: one I knew all too well.

"Where is your family, and why are you tied into all this?"

His face tightened. "Blaze N Fire is my family," he said, walking to me and snatching my arms to tie them back up.

I pulled my hands back. "Don't do this shit!" he gritted.

I stepped back, and he came forward. "Cortez is not going to show up. So, what am I supposed to do, let y'all kill me? Fuck no!"

I glanced at the door and then at him. Our eyes bounced on and off each other.

Run.

I hauled ass out the door and down the hall with him behind me. I spotted the front door, but his hand gripped my hair, pulling me back. "I told yo ass!"

He dragged me back into the room, tossing me on the floor and tying my hands back up.

"My father's a cop!" I screamed.

He instantly let me go.

"What?"

"I said my father is a cop. So, you better tell Lucas his ass is dead."

He stood staring at me. Now, his nerves were bad.

"Fuck, fuck, fuck!"

"And Diamond, that Zoo Boy you're looking for, you better watch out. I heard they are treacherous, and they're coming for you," I started to laugh hysterically.

I talked a lot of shit and hoped my words didn't bite me in the ass. I hoped it scared him enough to let me go.

DIAMOND- LAND

Malik had called me earlier, saying he wanted to talk about something, and my gut was telling me he wanted to end things. He and I had played this game before, so I was used to it. We've been dealing with each other since high school. I was hoping by now, he would have grown up. He thought by getting this condo it set the bar high for other niggas, and I was going to be all over him. *Wrong!* I needed more. I wanted a man who could provide in more ways than just financially. I saw how my mother gave up everything for my father, and I just wasn't that person. Malik figured I would move in with him, but I couldn't do it. I had great things going for me, and I didn't want anyone to pull me away from it.

When I came up the hall, I realized the same girl I fought with, and that was at the hospital, was the same girl that went off on me in the elevator over Diamond. When the shit clicked in my head, I couldn't believe it. Whatever type of dick he served her had her losing her mind. Seeing her coming from his place really placed Diamond at the bottom because, again, there had to be something there.

Diamond slammed his door, locking it behind him.

"What the hell!" I yelled.

He stood there in a towel. This man was so fine that I'd almost forgotten he snatched me inside. He hadn't said a word yet. His colored eyes bored into mine. I pulled my eyes away, taking in his place. The shit was nice as hell.

Snap, snap. "I'm over here," I heard him say.

Eyes on him. "You're standing there, not saying anything. Can you let me out, please? This shit is technically kidnapping!" I shouted.

He came a little closer. "No yelling unless I'm giving you something to yell for."

Closer.

He slightly leaned forward. "I don't give a fuck about what's technical or not. You can walk out that door if you want to, but I'm just going to pull your ass right back in here. You're right where you belong, in Diamond Land."

I rolled my eyes, tossing my hands on my hips. "Please."

Closer.

"Please, what?" he muttered.

Diamond had this swag about him that drew you in. Although you could tell he was toxic, his captivating behavior would swiftly draw you into his world. I didn't want to play in his chaotic amusement park. The shit was probably trash anyway. I went around him, heading to the door.

"What you running for?"

I wasn't running. I was simply going to the place I had intended to. My phone vibrated, and I knew it was Malik. He was probably wondering where I was.

I felt Diamond's body press against my back. My body stilled as I closed my eyes. He placed his lips to my ear, "I want you to stay, please," he whispered sweetly.

I turned around, and he still hadn't moved. He was so close there was barely space between us. "Diamond, you're in my face like a girl didn't just leave here. You're not about to play with me; now back the fuck up."

His lips grazed mine as he spoke, "You didn't tell me you had a nigga."

DIAMOND- LAND

"Yeah, well, you didn't tell me you had a girl, one that I fought remember; I don't have time for this shit move," I hissed.

Diamond did not budge. He stared into my eyes like he was searching for something. The more he stared, the more I was getting lost. His fingers stroked my cheek, sending love signals through my body. He was trying to break me down. He inched closer, running his soft lips up, pecking at the tip of my nose. He took two steps back. "Rayana, would you please stay? No, you're not mine yet," he paused. "I'd rather you chill with a real nigga than that nigga."

The nerve of him. "Wait, a real nigga is not having one woman leave, probably after fucking her and bringing another woman in his place. I don't know what kind of woman you think I am, but I'm not her. Now, bye, Diamond," I said as I turned to open the door to leave.

"Fuck Malik! Better tell that Roger-looking ass nigga to enjoy because tonight will be your last night going over there."

I just shook my head and walked out of the door. Diamond couldn't be serious. He wasn't even my man but was making demands. I knocked on Malik's door. When he answered, I put on a pretend smile. "Hey!"

Malik poked his head out of the door as if he was watching out for someone, then moved back to let me in. Walking into his place after leaving Diamond's was a completely different atmosphere. Malik barely had enough money to afford his rent, let alone buy things for his house. I was ok with it because I liked Malik for him, not what he had or didn't have. I set my purse on the small table he had in the living room. When I glanced at Malik, he seemed nervous and different. My gut told me I should have just gone home, but trying to be a good girlfriend, I brought my ass here.

"What's wrong?"

He shrugged his shoulders, "Nothing."

"You're lying, what's wrong?"

"I did a thing."

My eyes surveyed him curiously, "What thing, Malik?"

He was only upsetting me with the Mary-go-round bullshit. He came closer to me, lifting his shirt. Malik was more on the pretty boy side: no tattoos or piercings. However, when he lifted his shirt, there was a big ass BF brand on his stomach. My eyes widen, "Malik, you joined a fucking gang?"

He began laughing hysterically, "Hell nah, well, not technically."

I stepped closer to him and noticed a jacket lying over the back of the couch. My eyes bounced back on him. "You're in a biker crew?"

The man jumped up and down like a fucking kid. "Yes! Man, the shit so crazy, I had to do some wild shit to join, but

I'm here. Listen, I know I said I was saving to get you a ring, but I saw this bike and I—"

"The fuck! Malik, you can barely fucking pay rent, and you're out buying bikes? Fuck the ring because you were never going to buy it anyway."

I was in disbelief. He had never spoken of wanting to be a part of a fucking biker crew before, and suddenly his ass is the nighthawk. I was over him. There was no possibility of us moving forward. I snatched up my purse to leave.

"Wait, where are you going? I thought you would be happy for me."

"I am, just not for me. Malik, we're done."

"Damn, Rayana, that's selfish of you. I can see why you're lonely."

My head spun so fast toward him. "Lonely with your ass. I thought we were building toward something. You said you were saving for a ring, but the bike was more important, but I'm selfish? Fuck you and that bike."

"Fuck me? Fuck you! You're so goddamn stuck up, ain't like you give up the pussy like that, so what's the point?"

Now he had me fucked up. Malik was my first and the only guy I had ever been with. I was still learning things and wasn't comfortable in the bedroom yet, so sometimes I would hold out. However, him throwing it in my face only pissed me off. I drew my hand back to swing on his ass.

"Nah, Yana, you not doing that. Nigga, your best bet would be to never call her again. If you do, I will fill yo ass up with hot hollows," Diamond's voice filled the room.

Seeing him in this light was different. He was protecting me, and I had just turned him down. A part of me felt giddy inside but scared because I wasn't sure how this would end. Did Navi experience a side of Preach like this?

"Nigga how you get in here," Malik said.

"The same way I'm going to get in here and smoke yo ass if you talk to her like that again."

Malik gritted his teeth, lifting his shirt. "Fuck Zoo!"

Diamond slowly nodded. "Let me show you what Zoo do then nigga."

Diamond ran up to Malik, hitting him in the face. The pounding was endless, so forceful that I could have sworn I heard his bones crack. I knew although he had put on that player role, he was probably stressed the fuck out with everything going on between Chevy and Gloria. Malik was his relief. I ran up behind Diamond to pull him off. When he finally stopped, he lifted as his chest heaved in and out. "Fuck is you talking about fuck Zoo, bitch, Zoo over everything. Fuck Blaze N' Fire, nigga!"

Diamond turned, heading toward the door. He didn't bother to look at me. I glanced at Malik, who was lying on the floor, groaning in agony.

"Yana, let's go. I'm only saving you once. If you stay, you don't have to worry about me. Fuck that bitch nigga. He doesn't deserve you, so again, bring yo ass on," he gritted.

I didn't even hesitate; I took his hand, leaving Malik's place and going with Diamond.

The sounds of the bolted doors caught my attention. When it opened, the guard walked Chevy to the door, pointing to where I sat. He slowly eased up to the other side of the glass. We stared at each other for a few seconds without words. He flicked his nose, then sat down. I picked up the phone, and so did he.

"What's good?" Chevy said as he leaned back in the seat.

I felt like a disappointment. I hadn't slept since everything had went down. To know the woman I was in love with played a role in my nigga being locked up fucked with me. The

46

feeling that consumed me was much more aching than the feeling I had with my father. Chevy deserved so much, and it truly seemed like he was getting the fucked-up end of the stick.

Seeing him like this tore me apart. The guys wanted to come with me, but I felt like this visit was personal. It was me who was dealing with a woman whose father hated me so much he chose someone closest to me to snatch up. Chevy and I needed this talk.

"How are you holding up?"

"It's gone be what it is. This shit isn't going to stop my show."

I didn't know what words I wanted to use, but I knew I needed to say something, anything. "I'm sorry, my nigga. I swear on my life, I did not know they were going to arrest you," I said, barely above a whisper.

"I know," he paused as he had now leaned forward. "You love her?" he asked.

I felt choked up because despite him playing it cool, I knew Chevy, and it was probably fucking with his head. I cleared my throat, "Yes," I said, then blew out a deep breath. "I'm fucking in love with her, but—"

He stared at me and pointed. "Then love on her. I told y'all before my past is my past, and I don't want my world to affect yours. If she is the one for you Preach, do it, love her," he finished as he leaned back.

This shit was getting crazy. I didn't know what type of prayer I needed, but I was going to have to pull out the good book for it.

"What can I do as a friend?"

"Continue to be my friend. I want you to show that woman the same amount of love you show us. Preach, you have a heart of gold and sometimes, I wish I knew what that feels like."

"I don't want to preach at you, but talk to God, Chev. You don't have to have nobody around. Just you and him. Tell him what you want, what you need, ask him for forgiveness, and let him show you how great he is."

I stood to leave because there was much more I wanted to say, but considering where we were, I decided against it. Chevy called out to me before I hung up the phone. "Make sure shorty is for you, about you, and ride for you no matter what because that father of hers he ain't right," he said.

I trusted Chevy's word, but I already knew her father was an ass after seeing that fucked up ass haircut. I glanced at Chevy. "What happened with your pops?"

He didn't even look at me this time.

"They said the nigga got his toupee blown back," he said, looking around.

I said nothing more. I hung up, and so did he. He stood, walking back towards the guard. Watching him disappear into the back was heartbreaking. I knew it was time to get up with the crew. It was our chance to make shit right with Chevy. He needed us the most without asking. It was time to paint this bitch orange.

Preach told us he was going to see Chevy. He said he wanted to go alone, so we respected his wishes. I think a part of him felt worse because of Navi being a cop. I couldn't believe he'd never told us. If Preach trusted her, then we were going to back him. However, the idea of Chevy hating him for it, I'm sure played on his conscience

I needed today to clear my head. Although I could have spent the day alone, I wanted to spend it with Yana. The way Malik played her didn't sit right with me. After leaving his crib, I could have taken her back to my place and stroked her pretty pussy, making her forget him, but I wanted to do it right. *Diamond style.* The nigga Malik was a deadman walking speaking on the Zoo the way he did. I didn't know if I could fully trust Rayana yet, so killing the nigga in front of her wasn't an option. Her sister was already treading thin waters, and their daddy, that cornball ass nigga, still was on my radar.

I wanted to show her what a real man was like, so I'd texted her a location. She just put the thumbs up, and I was hoping she would show up. When I arrived at my lounge, I made sure everything was set. Dimmed lights, orange candles, chilled champagne, and music. I pulled my phone out of my pocket to see if she had texted back, but she hadn't.

I'd never been so anxious in my life. The sound of the door opening caught my attention. A pretty-ass smile eased on her face as she strolled my way in a cocoa-brown dress that complimented her well.

"Looking for me?"

I smiled and then licked my lips. "Yes, and I must say you look so fucking good."

"Thank you. It's so nice in here, did you do this by yourself?"

"Baby, it's my world. I do all of it by myself."

Rayana stepped closer to me with one leg in front and the other to the side. A whiff of her soft perfume whisked across my nose, sending my head flying to catch it. *One hand to her hip, the other to her ass.* I pulled her closer to me, staring into her eyes and finding myself getting lost in them.

"Diamond, are you tapping out?"

"Nah, baby, I'm tapping in. You're so fucking beautiful."

"You said that already."

"And a nigga will say it a million times more."

I wanted to kiss her. I wanted to lick her. I wanted the taste of her pussy on my palate. A nigga wanted to be inside her. I got my shit together as I took her hand, leading her to the table in front of the stage. She sat in the chair, crossing her legs. I walked over to the bar, grabbing flowers, "I know you said they were nice, but I think women should have flowers. Granny always said flowers make women smile, and a nigga love seeing you smile."

She giggled as she took the orange hydrangeas out of my hand. "You really love Ms. Gloria, don't you?"

"She's my life. She has given up a lot for me. I don't play when it comes to her. I will lose my mind the day God decides he wants her back," I said, feeling a tinge emotional talking about my granny.

"What about Chevy?"

Then anger struck me. "That's my nigga. I would die for him. He has been a savior. Speaking of that, yo sister bet not be on no shit either. I sang for her ass, and she's a cop. Why didn't you tell me?"

"Diamond, like you said, she's my sister. I will have her back before I have yours, and it's nothing against you; she's my family."

I was enjoying this open conversation. A woman had never really allowed me to talk to them this way. It had always been a sexual thing. So, to be able to talk to Yana felt nice.

"I get it, and how you feel about your sister is the same way I feel about Chevy. I would hate for us to turn bad before I had a chance to taste that pussy."

She shied away. I placed my fingers to her chin and turned her head my way. "What about that girl?" she mumbled

I knew she was talking about Mo. "Mo, she and I had something, something I thought was going good. She betrayed me and has been trying to get in my good graces ever since. I can handle a lot of things, Yana, but betrayal, I cannot."

Her eyes flickered. We stared at each other, taking in each other's energy. I wanted her badly.

"Let a nigga do something things to you. Shit yo daddy won't approve of."

Her eyes soften. "If I give my body to you that way, Diamond, there is no turning back," she whispered.

"Are you scared?" I asked, running my thumb across her lips.

"Yes."

"Hold that thought," I told her.

I backed away, getting on stage. I could see her laughing. I placed my lips to the mic, "Don't be over there laughing at me. I'd rather you be over there craving me."

I hit play on the instrumental and started. "*I don't know what you been told, but I know that I want you to put that pussy in my face,*" I started singing. "*I don't know what you been told, but I know that I want you to put that pussy in my face.*"

A loud laugh came from her belly. She stood slowly, strutting to the music as she came toward me. I hopped down, picked her up, and laid her back on the stage.

"Diamond, I've never let anyone do this before."

Peck to the lips, another, then another. "I think I'm about to tap out," I whispered.

She won. I wanted her. "Can I take you to Diamond Land?"

She nodded. "Baby, you have an all-access pass to me," I said as my tongue slid from the top of her forehead down to her lips.

My hands slowly slid up her thighs. "Diamond, I can't," she whispered as she pushed me off her. "I got to go," she mumbled, rushing out of the building.

Rayana was a different breed. She had a nigga wide open and ready. I was about to eat my fucking words because now I wanted to chase her.

His tall frame stood against the wall as he watched me watching him. Dark as midnight with no soul. He removed himself from the wall, pressing his firm palms on the mattress. My breathing became heavy. Was I scared? His crawl was slow, animal-like as he came closer toward me. His eyes were dark with hurt lingering in them. However, his presence was of royalty. He was a fucking king in his own right, and he knew it. Light growls came from his lips as he placed his finger to his lips signaling me not to say a word.

The aura around him sucked the air from my body into his. The deep dark waves in his hair were how my stomach felt. The shirtless mystery man ran his hands up the sides of my thighs connecting his energy with mine. I closed my eyes for a mere second only to open them with him directly in my face. Nose to nose, lips to lips. Our breathing heavy but in sync.

I'm going to save you. His mouth moved but I heard nothing.

The mystery man's hand moved from my outer thigh to my inner thigh. I inhaled deeply. "Just let me feel you," *he whispered.*

My head slowly nodded as his fingers made its way to my center. His fingertips grazed my clit barely touching me and my body shuddered. "What's your name?" *I asked.*

"It's—"

I felt my body jump. "Wake your snoring ass up!"

I hadn't realized I'd fallen asleep. The dream felt so real I didn't want it to end. Mystery man somehow invaded my dreams. I focused my attention on the person who had waken me and it was Lucas.

He stared at me like I had done something to him. "What?" I asked.

"Ace said your daddy is a cop, is it true?"

I mean he had long retired, but he didn't need to know all that. I would say whatever it took to get the fuck out of here. "Yes, he is and he's going to fuck you up!"

"What's the nigga name?"

"You should have done your homework since you know every fucking thing!" I spat.

He laughed loudly. "The bitch is a smarty pants," he gritted. "Ok smarty pants since you got all that mouth, let's see what you have to say when I put a fucking bullet in your head."

"Lonnie Richardson!" I screamed.

His face curled up. "Wait," he paused. "Your daddy is crooked ass Lonnie? Oh yeah, mama you're not going nowhere. Fuck yo daddy."

My Daddy wasn't crooked. He had done a lot for the community. He always gave back helping young black men all the time.

"That's a lie," I said to him.

Lucas shook his head. "Oh, you were a sheltered bitch. You don't know him like I do. Your father the same nigga that use to come around shaking *young black niggas* up for money threatening to take they ass down to county if they didn't pay," he said pacing the floor. "Your father the same nigga that was working with that white man who we later found out was crooked as well trying to run for council winning the black people's vote. You got it all wrong baby girl. Your Daddy is a bitch!" he barked.

The things he was saying couldn't be true. My Daddy was a hero to many. He closed the most cases in his department. He fucking help get people out of jail. I was so confused. However, if what he was saying was true, he'd truly fooled all of us and most of all Navi who looked up to him. I sat there with my head down because I simply did not want to believe what he was saying.

His loud clap made my head snap up. "Now that we got that out the way. Tonight, it's Blaze N Fire vs Zoo. Ace, I want you to take that nigga's bike and bring it to the downtown bridge. Let's end the animal boys," he laughed. "And you," he pointed to me. "Cortez has two fucking days to show his face or you're going to be in somebody's cold storage."

Lord, please let them be looking for me, please.

CHAPTER FOUR

PREACH

We Got A Problem

It was time to link up with the guys to shake shit up. I really needed to figure this shit out with Chevy and Navi's fathers because I wanted to move forward with her without this hanging over my head. The goal was to figure out Chevy's situation first so we could get him out. Once that was done it would be me versus Mr. Richardson. I knew he was upset about how things played out at dinner, but I tried being nice. Hell, I gave him some encouraging scriptures. It was clear he didn't apply them because his ass was out here being the devil's bitch.

DIAMOND- LAND

I sent out a text to my niggas because I needed to make sure that they were on board.

Message
(Today) PM 2:30

> Orange Village in an hour.

I'm in the middle of something I will be there. We got to talk anyway.

I see this the chat without Chev. It has to be serious. OMW.

> Yes it is.

Man who I got to shoot. I don't have time for the small talk.

Damn Foe, chill my nigga. Blazin' glory ass nigga.

I'm bringing Harvey and I don't want to hear a fuck thing!

> Nigga, chill when the time is right we will.

> Whatever nigga just be there!

Message
(Today) PM 2:35

 So what y'all made up?

 None of yo business. Don't you have better shit to do than be worried about who I'm dealing with.

Diamond stop playing nigga.

 Zu nigga stop crying like a bitch, I'm about to eat then I will be there!

 Interesting. Make sure you keep her close my nigga. Can't be slipping up.

Ha fuckin ha. Now all of a sudden y'all the love doctor. Fuck y'all I'm omw.

I'm gone pray for y'all niggas.

When they all responded, I headed to the Orange Village. If my plan worked, I knew there would be hope for Pretty and me. The storm God was brewing up was near, and I could feel it in my spirit. I was ready and needed to get my niggas ready too.

"Oh my- my, *God!*" Rayana moaned loudly.

I had her sprawled across the bed with my face smothered between her legs. The sweet taste of Yana's pussy in my mouth made a nigga want to go harder. It took a minute to convince her to let a nigga taste her, but here we were. I felt her hand go to my head as she took a handful of my hair, shoving my face closer to her clit. My nose pressed against her pussy. I was determined to suck the soul from her little ass. I lapped around, then slurped.

"Diamond, please st-stop. I can't," she whined.

I could tell she was fresh and never had a nigga's mouth on her cause baby was going crazy. Lifting one of her legs over my shoulder, I pulled her further down. I knew I was supposed to meet up with the guys, but pleasing her in this moment was a priority. I could tell she wasn't being loved on properly, and I wanted to be the nigga to show her that there were good men out here. Yana's body bucked, then shook.

"Something is happening, Diamond, ah!" she screamed.

Her juices flowed from her into my mouth, and I slurped every fucking drop up. When I pulled away from her, I stood as she gazed at the ceiling, panting hard.

"I did something to you, that nigga Malik ain't never done," I told her.

Once she calmed down, she pulled herself up. "We can't do this again," she mumbled.

"Why?" I asked as I headed to the bathroom.

I grabbed a warm towel, making my way back to her. She went to grab the towel, and I pulled back.

"Let me. I made the mess; let me clean it up." I winked.

I eased her back slightly, then opened her legs, cleaning her up. I could see her blushing, and when she caught me looking, she stopped. "I can be a gentleman. I know how to treat women," I told her.

Once I was done, she stood up and swiftly slipped her panties back on, followed by her pants. "Diamond, I cannot let you do that again. I shouldn't have let you do it in the first place."

She was tripping. I knew Rayana liked me as much as I liked her, but something about her playing this tough role was tripping me out. I'd never had a woman tell me I couldn't eat her pussy. However, I wasn't about to keep playing cat and mouse.

"Fine, I don't know what type of games you playing, but I'm not with it. I want to spend time with you, I want to cuddle with you, hell a nigga want to fuck you, but if we have to do all this, I don't want it," I told her.

She moved around the room while I went into the bathroom to get cleaned up and ready.

"It's not that I don't want you. I just want to one: make sure you and that girl are completely done, and two, I don't want to be some nigga's play toy!" she yelled.

I poked my head out of the bathroom door, "Stop yelling in my shit. Me and her are not together, so what the fuck?"

"Like I said, we're not doing this again."

"Like I said, fine."

Her phone started going off. The old me wouldn't have cared, but something in me told me it was Malik's ass. I came from the bathroom, and she snatched up her purse walking out of my room.

"Where are you going?"

She spun around to face me. "I have to work, so I'm leaving."

Her phone went off again. She looked down at the phone, then at me. *It had to be that bitch ass nigga.* I was two seconds from grabbing my gun to go shoot his shit up. Maybe she had some type of nigga elixir in her pussy because suddenly I didn't even want her to leave.

She swung the door open and then looked at me. "Exactly nigga!"

Rayana brushed past Mo, who was standing at the front door, looking simple as hell. *Fuck!*

"Diamond, I'm really not here to—"

I dropped my head. "I don't want to hear shit, Mo. You have to stop!" I barked.

"Diamond, please listen to me."

I snapped. "*No!*" I shouted as my voice bounced off the hall walls. "A nigga tried being nice by telling you to leave me the fuck alone. I tried giving you some dick to leave me alone, and you keep coming around. Monette," I said, now moving closer to her. "Leave. Me. The. Fuck. Alone," I finished, closing the door in her face.

I was pissed she even popped up. The more she did the shit, the more I regretted even serving her the piece of dick I did. It took me another ten minutes to get ready and leave the house. I really wanted Mo to back off because she was becoming a problem. She was leaving me no choice but to off her ass if she didn't stop.

"Man, Malik, yo scary ass coming with me. You said the nigga lives across from you!" Ace spat.

He and Malik had been going back and forth for the last twenty minutes about them trying to steal from the Zoo Boyz. I knew very little about them other than the one my sister had fallen for, and the other was one who always seemed to be in the right place at the right time. I wished he'd somehow magically appear now, but since he hadn't, I needed to make this work to survive.

"I'll help you," I jumped in. "I will help you if you at least let me tell my family bye," I said to Ace.

Malik glared at me. "No!" he spat.

I rolled my eyes, "Malik, does Rayana know you're here? Does she know the man she has been with for these last few years is out here playing cat and fucking robbers?"

He stared me down. Ace swung him by his arm, "Nigga you fucking her sister?"

"Nah, that bitch tripping, she doesn't know what she's talking about, and if I was, her sister wasn't worth the fuck."

My head flew back because he was not about to play with Rayana like that. "Says the same nigga I caught climbing through her window begging her for pussy. The nerve. I hope she leaves your ass!"

Ace glanced at me, then at Malik. "For someone who is on the brink of death, you have a whole lot of mouth. It's either you're really about that life, or you're so scared shit talking is all you can do," Ace said to me.

He walked over to me, standing me up. "I'm taking you with me."

"Lucas is going to flip," Malik rushed over to Ace.

"Lucas is also pussy footing around trying to make decisions. Besides, he said he wanted the super nigga, let's see if we can get him to come out."

Ace walked me out of the room, and I stopped. "Wait, I said let me call my family."

He yanked my arm, "I got you, but you're going to help me first. If you try something, then *boom!* One to the back of your head."

I swallowed deep as he led me outside and into the car. Malik ran out, hopping in the back seat with me. "Ain't no way I'm letting you take her alone," he told Ace. He then leaned over to my ear. "Fuck your raggedy ass sister."

Little did they know the first chance I got, I was hauling ass.

"Finally!" Harvey yelled.

"Damn, zookeeper, were you waiting?"

"Fuck you!"

"That's Zu's job."

Zu turned my way, "Nigga you better chill; this is your last warning."

I cackled. "Diamond cut the shit," Preach jumped in.

I was the one that needed to be uptight, but I was trying my best to keep a clear head before I lost my shit, and the only way I could do that was by joking around. I glanced at Preach, who looked like he was ready for war. "We need to find out about Chevy's pops. We need to know what happened."

Foe turned to him, "You heard what he said. The nigga fucked with him, and he snapped."

"But years later? It's not making sense. If that were the case, why wouldn't he do it then?"

Everybody turned to Harvey as she walked over, sitting on Zu's lap. I glanced at Foe. Something caught my attention. There was an unsettling aura around him. I watched how he looked at Harvey. Shit was weird, or maybe I was just tripping because of my situation. I focused back on Harvey like everyone else.

"Why are y'all looking at me?"

"Bae, you're the closest to the nigga other than myself, and he never told me about this shit," Zu said to her.

"Bae? Oh, nigga she got you soft as a bitch!" I blurted out.

"Or you just mad you don't have a Bae 'Cause yo hoe ass can't keep a chick," Harvey snapped back.

I could keep a woman if she was worth keeping. Then Rayana popped into my head. I pulled out my phone to send her a text, and the shit bounced back. "*Man, shit!*" I mumbled.

"What?" Preach asked.

"Nothing, keep talking."

Now, I felt like Harvey was right. *Could I not keep a woman for real? Or is it I hadn't really tried?*

"Even if I knew something, why would I tell y'all? Don't get me wrong, I fuck with you guys, but my loyalty is with Chev," she said, now standing from Zu's lap.

This time I caught her staring at Foe like they were mentally speaking to each other, and he told her to get her ass up. I had to be tripping.

"All we want to do is help him. Navi said—"

"Fuck her!" Harvey shouted.

"Just fucking listen!" Preach yelled.

I'd never heard the nigga raise his voice before. He had to be stressed.

"We all know Chevy, and he doesn't give a fuck about the law. He's already determined to take this trip; what goes to say he won't run? Now, Navi said," he paused, looking at Harvey. "That all we need to do is figure out what the fuck happened so we can get them off his back. I tried asking the nigga, but he wouldn't say shit. So, Harvey, sweetheart, if you know anything, please tell us," he said, walking up to her. "And Navi, that's my girl, and if you two are going to be in the same space, because she will be around, I need you to respect her," he finished.

My nigga Preach was in love. I'd never seen him this way before. Harvey slowly nodded her head.

"All I know is he used to torture Chev in what way, I don't know. When he got older, Chevy had invested all his money in a business only for his father and his partner to take the business from under him, leaving him with nothing," She glanced at Zu. "The reason he was so upset at what you did, putting his business up, is because he had worked so hard to get it up and running legally. This is the only thing I can think of. Chevy has a lot of demons."

Now shit started to make sense of why he was the way he was. Knowing what he did only made Zu look worse. I could tell the situation was still fucking with Zu, and there were no words we could say to change the shit he did. He would have to find a way to fix the situation.

"I will figure out who the partner is, and once I do. Y'all already know."

Foe nodded with a sinister grin, "Happy on the fucking trigga," he said.

I cleared my throat. "We have another problem," I told them.

"Ah, shit!" Foe said.

Preach dropped his head, exhaling loudly, "Lord, I'm trying," he said as he pinched the bridge of his nose. "What is it?"

"Blaze N' Fire. We have to put them niggas down. I had to beat a nigga's ass the other night for talking shit."

Zu held his hand out, "Wait, we raced and smoked they ass already. Why would the nigga be talking shit."

I felt like all eyes were on me. "I was saving somebody. She needed my help."

"Chevy already saved a girl, and that's how we ended up racing them in the first place," Zu said.

My mind got to going. *Was Rayana fucking with Chevy?*

"What girl? What's her name?" I asked.

Zu shrugged. Now my head was fucked up because if it was Rayana he was speaking about, I could no longer fuck with her if she was fucking with Chevy. I went to say something else when I noticed a call coming in from the hospital. I stood up, walking out of the door.

"Hello?"

"Hi, Mr. Blanco, this is the nurse here at—"

"I know, is my granny, ok?"

"Yes, about Gloria, there is someone here who is advising you no longer have rights to see Ms. Gloria. Normally, we wouldn't call, but I know how much you—"

"The fuck is you talking about someone said I can't see my granny? Lady, I'm not in the mood for games."

"Mr. Blanco, I didn't have to call, but I did. You may need to speak to an attorney and have them provide power of attorney, and fast."

Everything in my mind went blank. All that shit she was talking was Spanish to me. I didn't even bother to tell my boys I was leaving; I rushed to my car. I saw Dio pulling up as I zoomed past him. My only thought was about the one person I loved, and that was my fucking granny.

CHAPTER FIVE

YANA

who is Grandma G

I felt like such a fool after leaving Diamond's. Not only because I allowed the man to put his mouth on me, but because I stooped so low, feeling like I needed to prove something to Diamond based on what Malik said the other night. Then, only to get slapped in the face when that girl showed up yet again. All of it reminded me why I needed to stay the course and focus on myself and not a man. *Diamond Land, tuh!* I can't lie and say what he was doing to my body didn't feel like a piece of heaven, but that was the problem. I felt like he couldn't feel beyond sex. He was a pure hoe, and I fell into his trap.

DIAMOND- LAND

"Shit!"

Malik was blowing up my phone, calling me back-to-back. He probably thought I would come running back because he and I had played that game before. I was done. That night he proved to me I meant nothing to him. I sped down the highway, trying to get to work, when he called again.

I picked up this time. "Hello!" I shouted.

"You better leave that nigga alone because he's dead."

"Now you're talking stupid. Malik please."

He laughed. "Rayana, I'm gone smoke that nigga I promise," he said and hung up.

I didn't know if it was jealousy or he was upset Diamond beat his ass, but I didn't want to risk it. I unblocked Diamond's number and tried calling, but he didn't answer. I just needed to remind myself after work to call him.

When I pulled up to the hospital, something in me told me to text Zari. I hadn't spoken to her in a while, and I wanted to hear from her. I sent her a text as I exited my car, rushing into the hospital. When I reached my floor, I saw Diamond going back and forth with the front desk worker. I rushed over, stepping to the side of him.

"Diamond," I called out, but he wouldn't look at me. "Diamond!" I shouted this time.

Eyes on me. The pain in his eyes was one I wasn't expecting. Immediately, I knew it was about Gloria. I glanced at the nurse. Seeing him like this further let me know telling him about his friend was a big ass no.

"What's going on?" I asked.

"He can no longer go back there."

Diamond bit into his bottom lip, "I'm going back there. Fuck is you talking about. That's my granny," he slapped his palm against his chest.

I placed my hands to his chest, pushing him back. "Diamond please, let me find out what's going on. I need you to calm down before they kick you out and then you won't be welcome back, trust me," I said to him.

"I don't trust nobody," he gritted.

Eyes on me. Trust me, please. I mouthed.

I placed both hands to his face. This time, when our gazes met, there was a shift in the atmosphere, leaving me with an indescribable sensation. His serious demeanor sent a shiver down my spine. It was becoming increasingly clear that I was developing feelings for him.

"Man, if something happens to my—"

"Nothing will happen I will take care of her, but I need you to calm down."

"If I can't go back there Yana, I'm painting this bitch red. I swear fo' Jesus. She's not just my granny, that's my momma," he choked up.

I could feel my emotions taking a toll on me. "Listen, I got you, like you had me the other night, remember?" I told him. "I will be right back, stay here," I finished.

I slowly eased away from him as I headed toward the back. When I checked Gloria's records, I noticed he requested her to be moved to a private room. I headed toward the room and when I stepped inside, there was a lady sitting on the side of her. Gloria looked at me and smiled. "This my favorite nurse," she said.

"Ms. Gloria, how are you feeling girl?" I smiled back.

The lady watched me curiously.

"Hi, I'm Rayana the night shift nurse."

"Chew, Chew likes her too. Where is Chew?"

"Momma I told you already that boy is not your grandson."

My heart felt like it had stopped. What did she mean? I wanted to ask so many questions, but I knew I needed to keep it professional.

"He's been in here every day. Ms. Gloria said—"

She cut me off. "My mother is old. I know what I'm talking about. Once I get clearance she is going with me. I don't know who this Diamond Blanco is, but he is not kin to her," she spat.

"Diamond Blanco is the one footing the bill for *your* mother. He is the same man that has been up here every day since *your* mother had a heart attack making sure she is okay. So, give him credit for something," I said back to her.

I knew it wasn't my place, but I also knew how much he cared for her.

"Yeah, well, I'm here now," as she rubbed Gloria's leg.

"Let him at least say goodbye," I mumbled.

She sat back in the seat. I watched her. She looked like she was trying to present herself as if she held a distinguished lifestyle. I was curious if she had cared so much for her mother. Why was it Diamond who was here since day one instead of her? I glanced at Gloria, and it seemed like her thoughts were outside of the window she was looking out of. For the most part she was good, but I knew a part of her mind was gone. My eyes landed back on her daughter. *Synthetic wig, chipped toenail polish, nervous demeanor.* She was faking this shit. She was probably waiting for something to happen to Ms. Gloria so she could get whatever money she could. She didn't give me a true, concerned daughter. However, she still had rights over her mother.

"Bring him back here. I want to talk to this Diamond that has been pretending to be her grandson."

I swallowed deep. I smiled, then nodded as I headed out of the door; I knew I needed to prepare Diamond for a huge war he was about to walk into. I just needed him to know I had his back through it.

After the meeting with the guys, I tried calling up Pretty. The lack of communication between us since Chevy's arrest made me realize how much I missed her.

"Hey baby," she cooed.

A warm feeling came over me. It was like I could breathe hearing her voice. "Where are you?"

I could tell she was smiling on the other side of the phone, "Leaving work, did you find out anything?" she asked.

I knew Pretty wanted to help to win my heart, but she already had it. Whether she could do anything or not, my heart was hers. I knew she probably didn't believe me when I said I was putting her Daddy down, but I was. Right now, I didn't want to talk about it. I wanted to make the time we did have about us.

"Just that his dad had a partner and from what I gather them muhfucka's were scheming against Chevy."

"Hmm, you know this partner's name?" she asked.

"No, but you know we will find out. I'm on my way, go home," I told her.

"Why?"

"Because I said so, now get there. I'm on my way."

I hung up with Pretty. I meant what I said when I told her we were done having sex until we were married, but it didn't mean I couldn't have a meal or two. I turned to Foe who was sitting at the table, "I'm out, hit me if y'all find out anything."

"Blaze N fire what we gone do about them?"

"Find them niggas, take them to the Zoo, hit me when you do," I told him.

As I headed out of the Orange Village, Dio was coming in.

"Sup Preach, where is Zeus?" Dio asked.

"In the back," I said.

I left, heading to see Pretty. I hopped on my bike taking off. I thought about everything that had transpired since meeting Pretty. How God placed her in my life so unexpectedly. She really should have been an op, but somehow turned into the love of my life. Maybe she was placed in my life not just for me, but for the crew. Pretty was more beneficial than she knew. The sad part of it all was I was going to break her heart.

After giving my sermon, I knew I didn't have to be confined to the church to be the person I was. Me and God had our own relationship and when the time was right, I would be where I needed to be.

God had put me here to be a savior to someone and I believe it was Chevy. Just so happened he had also given me an obstacle, and that was Pretty. I felt like it was a test to see if I could truly forgive someone without malice in my heart.

By the time I pulled up to Pretty's, I noticed another car there. I felt in my spirit; it was about to get nasty. I got off my bike walking up to her door. I dropped my head. "Lord, please forgive me for what I'm about to do, Amen."

I knocked on the door and waited. Sure enough, when the door opened, he was standing there. We were eye to eye. I smirked, then glanced over his shoulders, looking at Pretty.

Preach, please don't. she mouthed.

"I see you still coming around my daughter."

"Sir, I'm going to be around for fucking ever, if you have a problem with it that's between you and the man upstairs," I replied.

He shrugged his shoulders, glancing back at Pretty, then me. Between the fucked-up haircut and the shitty ass smirk he had on his face was enough to trigger me.

"My daughter is a cop, one that doesn't need any likings of—"

Whap!

I hit his ass in his mouth. "Preach!" Navi screamed.

Her Daddy flew back into the house. *Whap!* Another one to his big ass nose. "I tried Mr. Richardson," I said, stepping into her house and closing the door behind me.

I kicked the nigga in his stomach. "You forced my hand and now I got to show you the man you want me to be. A hood nigga, right?"

Stomp!

"Some ghetto piece of shit!" I barked.

Stomp!

"Preach, please," Navi cried.

I glanced up at her as tears poured out of her. It made me stop. I stepped over him, walking up to her, tapping her nose. I leaned into her ear, "It's going to happen. Spend these last few days with this nigga. Have your last supper and say your goodbyes," I finished, kissing her on the cheek.

"I'm going to have you arrested just like I did with June Calloway," he grunted.

84

It took the army of the lord for me to not pull my gun out on his ass. The way I wanted to end him it was something I didn't need Pretty playing in her head over and over. I walked out of the house with a tight face. I wasn't worried about being arrested because if his daughter loved me enough, she would stop him. I was about to shake some shit up, though. I left Pretty's house with no further words.

I stood there waiting for Yana to come back. I paced the floor back and forth, trying to comprehend what the hell was going on. Me not being able to see my granny was fucking with me. It had been me and her for as long as I could remember. When I did my bid, I promised once I got out, I would never leave her again. My grandmother was practically my fucking mother. She was my soul. I needed answers, and I wanted them today.

Yana had an aura about her that gave me some form of peace and that alone spoke volumes. I glanced up the hall, and she was walking toward me. As she got closer, her face told me shit still wasn't right.

"Don't tell me shit I don't want to hear." Yana, I can't I—"

She reached out to me, "Diamond, I need you to listen to me ok," she said calmly. "I'm going to take you back there. You need to act like you got some sense because the shit that is about to hit you is going to make you snap."

"I don't give a fuck!" I yelled.

"Diamond!" she yelled. "Look at me, I'm fucking serious. This is about Gloria not you so, please. Just know I'm here with you the entire way through," she finished.

Then she did something that changed not just my mood, but made me look at her differently. She slid her fingers between mine. The shit may seem corny, but it made me feel good. To know she was in my corner made a nigga feel like she cared. We walked down the hall until we reached the door to the room. She squeezed my hand making me look down at her. *I got your back.* She mouthed.

As soon as I stepped into the room, my granny called out to me, "Chew!"

I let Yana's hand go rushing over to my granny, embracing her in a hug. "I love you, Granny," I whispered in her ear.

"I know Chew, Chew, I love you too,"

"Uh hmm," I heard.

When I glanced over, there was a lady standing there who I'd never seen before. She looked just like my granny, just younger. She and I stared at each other for a few minutes before I heard Yana's voice.

"Diamond, this is—"

"I don't need you to introduce me, I'm—"

"Who you talking to, huh? You don't speak to her you speak to me, ma'am," I snapped.

"I'm ok, Diamond," Yana whispered.

"Like I said," she stepped closer to me. "I'm Constance Gaylord and Gloria Gaylord is my mother." She smirked.

I'd never heard of her, granny never talked about her. She never had photos around the house, so she had to be lying. "Lies," I said back.

"I am her only daughter. She has no other kids. What I'm trying to figure out is who are you and why you have my mother believing you are related to her when you're not?"

All the shit sounded like a blur. I turned toward my granny, "What is she talking about Granny? Huh?"

I looked at Constance, then back at my granny. When my granny looked at me, her eyes changed. The shit was true. I could feel myself about to blow a fucking lid. I felt Yana's hands on mine, but I snatched it away. I rushed to my granny's side, "If this is true then who am I? Where the fuck are my parents? Granny you lied to me? Huh!" I shouted.

"Diamond, calm down," I heard Yana say.

I wanted to, I really did, but this shit was too much. This was the only lady I knew, and to hear this shit had been a lie. I couldn't control my emotions.

"Granny!"

"She's not—"

"Shut the fuck up, lady! He knows that, let him process it," Yana stepped in.

"I want him out of here now. Diamond I'm not sure where your parents are but she's not it."

I blacked out. "Fuck you mean! This is my fucking granny, she raised me. Your Wanda looking ass come up in here trying to change shit. Got a nigga confused," I went off.

I felt a pair of hands on me, "Get the fuck off me. Granny!" I called out.

She turned to look at me and a tear slid down her cheek and I broke free, rushing to her. *Hands to my arms.* I swung.

Whap! Whap! Whap!

I began pounding on the security. I couldn't hear shit. More security came in, carrying me out. I saw Yana's mouth moving like she was screaming but couldn't hear shit. It was all a fucking blur. They dragged me out of the room and down the hall. They had me so tight I couldn't move. They carried me all the way out of the hospital.

"Sir you need to leave the premises before we call the cops!"

"Fuck you, bitch nigga! Fuck you!" I shouted.

I felt empty. I felt alone. I walked away, not knowing who I really was, and that hurt the most.

We had sat in the car right outside of the Orange Village for what seemed like hours. I'd never been to the Zoo Boyz territory but being in their neck of the woods the energy was heavy. Something was telling me none of this was going to go the way they planned it. Ace sat in the driver seat peeping out of the window every other minute. I wasn't sure what he was waiting on, but I was becoming restless.

I felt a hand sliding up and down my thigh, I glanced over at Malik who had been getting high the entire ride looking at me raising his brows, "If you don't get your hands off of me, I'm going to snap."

Ace turned to look at him, "Nigga this isn't the time to cop a feel. I'm going to run over there to take that bike, Malik, I need you to drive and smart mouth you're going to be the lookout."

If he really thought, I was going to help him he had me fucked up. Before he could get out two other members pulled up. He looked at Malik, "Nigga you called them?"

"Hell, yeah, I did. Them niggas got guns we need back up."

They had both gotten out of the car and a different person got in the driver seat. I was thinking of a way I could run from his ass, but the way Ace had me tied up I could barely move. I was hoping like hell he'd let me go with him. I pressed my face against the window watching them as they ran into the parking lot disappearing.

"Shit I got to piss," I heard the guy in the driver seat say.

He got out of the car walking only a few steps away. It was now my time to run. I scooted back, leaned forward grabbing the door handle with my mouth opening it. I scooted until I was out of the car. I couldn't believe I was about to run. The shit was like a fucking movie. As soon as I stood up, I heard gunshots.

Bloaw! Bloaw!

Run.

I hauled ass. The wind smacked me in the face as I made my way down the street. *Turn right. Cross the street. Red light. Turn left.* I was running so fast I didn't know where I was going. I went to cross the street again when a car stopped only inches from hitting me.

"Help, please!" I shouted.

When the person emerged from the car. I knew right then the universe had it out for me because of all people it was fucking Cortez!

I got the text that they had found some of the niggas from Blaze N Fire and they had them at the Zoo. I'd been reaching out to Diamond, but the nigga was ghost. Tension was building outside the crew, and I believed everybody was losing their shit. I pulled up to the Zoo with a million things going through my head. I needed to set up the play on Navi's dad, and figure out if they were going to let my nigga Chevy out on bail. Zu still hadn't come up with a name and I was ready to say fuck it and burn this bitch down. When I walked inside there were four niggas hanging. "Somebody's dying today!" Zu howled.

DIAMOND- LAND

"Ah, shit!" Foe spat.

I clapped my hands as I got closer. "Blaze and fucking Fire."

I watched as three of them squirmed with fear and one hung holding his chin. I knew immediately that nigga was the strongest of the bunch. The sound of Diamond's voice caught our attention. As he came into the light, I could tell something was wrong. I just reminded myself to ask later.

Clap! Clap!

Diamond clapped his hands so loud the sound echoed throughout the warehouse. He tossed his hair in a ponytail stepping closer to the niggas hanging. He pointed at one of them. "Let his ass down!" He barked.

I'd never seen him this angry before. We were always used to him joking and playing around, seeing this side of him we didn't know how to respond. Nobody moved.

"Fuck it I'll do it myself," he gritted as he snatched the knife from the table, hopping on it, and slicing the rope sending the nigga slamming against the ground.

"Damn warrior we see you," Foe said to Diamond.

He jumped off the table going in. He raised his leg slamming his foot down on the side of the nigga's face.

"I warned yo ass," he growled.

Stomp!

"Malik, I never liked yo corny ass!"

Whap! Whap!

"*Oo shit!* Diamond shaking shit up!" Zu howled like a wolf.

Whap! Whap!

"A thousand pounds of pressure on yo ass," Diamond said leaning down in the nigga's face.

Stomp!

He walked over to the table snatching the gun. I ran up to him. "Nigga, you aight?"

"Always," he said as he aimed the gun at the side of the nigga's head.

I knew it was a lie because it was a term we all used when we were really going through shit and didn't want people to know.

"Y'all out here trying to steal from some niggas you know nothing about. I warned you, Malik. Now like I said before let me show you what Zoo do and Rayana, that pussy is mine. I can still taste her on my palate, nigga."

Bloaw!

Diamond sent a single bullet into the side of his head. He stood turning toward the other niggas. He aimed but Foe ran up to him. "Slow down sharpshooter, save some for us. What the fuck is up?" Foe asked.

Diamond was breaking down by the second. "My fucking granny dawg," he muttered.

Zu stepped up. "Before we even get into that. Let's handle these niggas first then we'll talk."

"Agreed," I said.

I turned to the three hanging. "Have any of you prayed today?"

"Nigga ain't nobody praying. If you gone kill us, then do that shit!" one of them spat.

"Fine!"

Pop, pop, pop!

Foe sent three bullets in his ass, sending the nigga's body swinging back and forth. One began wailing loudly while the other hung there still with no words. "Man, it was Lucas!" the crying little nigga said.

"Man shut yo ass up!" the other gritted.

Zu stepped up to him sending a fierce blow to his stomach knocking the wind out his ass. "Keep talking little nigga before I shoot you," Zu told him.

"Lucas is on a war path. One of your niggas saved this bitch and now he wants his money back. An-an-and—"

Clap!

Foe clapped his hands. "Come on now stuttering Stanley we don't have all goddamn day."

"And he wants that nigga to come see him."

"Oh, he wants smoke from Chev," I nodded. "Smoke from Chev. Sounds like yo boy is heavy on Chevy, well too bad cause the nigga is not here!" I roared.

Just him bringing my nigga up had me riled up.

"Yeah, that nigga and you, Diamond, he said you killed his brother, Rock."

We turned to Diamond who looked at us. Zu stepped up, "Wait, is he talking about the nigga that Chev smoked the night we saved you?"

Diamond nodded. "Well too bad," Diamond said.

Bloaw! Bloaw! Bloaw! Bloaw!

Foe ran up, "Damn chill on the trigger the nigga is dead."

"Let that other nigga down," I instructed.

They all stared at me. "Preach what the fuck you been smoking. We're not letting this nigga down," Foe spat.

"Nah, I want him to go back to Lucas, is it?"

The nigga nodded. "Tell him the Zoo is coming for him and it's war!"

They let the nigga down and he wasted no time hauling ass right out of the warehouse. "Heavenly Father, I pray they found peace before they took their last breath, Amen."

Now it was time to set up Pretty's Daddy, and I knew I would need Diamond's help, but first, we all needed to talk about what was going on with him.

It had been three days since seeing Diamond. Although I was out of line at work for what I did, I was able to continue to help Ms. Gloria and I think it was solely because she was comfortable with me. I felt so bad after the incident with Diamond. I wanted to call and check on him, but I felt like seeing him would be better.

I was on my way to Navi's because I hadn't seen her in a while. I was hoping she and I could head to Zari's since she had been ignoring my text and calls. As I drove to her place, I noticed she was calling me.

"Ray!" she yelled.

I curled up my face as I looked at the phone before putting it back up to my ear, "Hey, Navi."

"I've been blowing you up. Have you talked to Zari?"

"No isn't she on house arrest. Did you go over there?"

"Yes! She's not fucking here. The bracelet is on the bed," she said panicking.

Zaria had always been clever at getting herself out of situations. So, it didn't surprise me that she got out of the bracelet, but to be gone was another story. Then I thought about her trying to steal her shit back from Cortez. The feeling I had in my gut told me something wasn't right. A sense of panic consumed me.

"Stay there I'm on my way!" I shouted, hanging up.

I took a quick turn hopping on the highway doing eighty in a sixty. I got to her house in no time. By the time I reached the door, it was open. I spotted Navi sitting on the couch, staring at the bracelet.

"Her fucking drawers are open like she was in a rush, or did someone stage it to look that way," she mumbled.

"Check her location, call her phone."

"I did, nothing and her location is off."

I pulled my phone out, "I'm calling Daddy!"

"Fuck that, we're going to see Cortez!"

Navi's eyes glared at mine. She was ready to fuck some shit up and I was with all of it. I knew a part of her felt guilty for not helping Zari when she asked. Hell, I felt guilty too; I didn't think she would really do it. Navi shot up from the couch as we both rushed out. She hopped in my car, and I took off. As I dove in and out of the lanes, Navi rocked back and forth in the seat. By the time I reached Cortez's she didn't even let me park before jumping out. I quickly placed the car in park in the middle of the street jumping out and running behind her. She knocked on the door. "Navanna please I'm kicking this bitch in!" I yelled.

I took a few steps back, throwing my leg out only for the door to open, causing me to kick the person, and sending them flying back. Navi rushed in drawing her gun on the girl who answered. "Where the fuck is my sister bitch!"

The girl frantically threw her hands up, "She asked you a question hoe!" I shouted.

Navi moved through the house like a detective, she tossed and move shit around dipping in and out of the rooms. "Please! If this is about Cortez, he isn't here. He left days ago and hasn't been back," she cried.

Navi came back, pointing the gun at her again, "If the nigga comes back, you tell him Navanna is on his ass like white on rice and I will be the fuck back. I should burn this bitch down!" she gritted.

"What she said," I jumped in.

I rushed behind my sister. I haven't seen her like this since we were young, and some girl stole my bike. I knew Navi wouldn't go to our father. She was going to find Zari on her own, but I knew we needed the help.

"Navi, maybe we can ask Preach to help us. They're street niggas I'm sure they can find her,"

She stopped walking, turning to me, "He's not going to do that. Daddy did some shady shit, and I know. I feel it. Preach doesn't trust me. Between Zari and Daddy putting me in a situation. I may lose the man that I fucking love. So, no I cannot ask him. I will find her though," she finished getting into the car.

I could see in my sister's eyes she was hurting and that made me hurt. However, I was going to get the help we needed. Either Diamond or Chevy was going to help me. I was going to start with Chevy. If he wanted my silence, he was going to have to do something for me.

My knees bounced up and down as I sat waiting for them to bring Chevy out. I felt like my world was crumbling before me and I needed the only person that I felt could steer me right before I lost my shit. They had finally brought him out. When he saw me, he picked up the phone before even sitting down.

"Grandma G straight?"

I blew out a deep breath. "Chev, my nigga I'm about to lose it."

He placed both elbows on the slate. "Diamond, calm down and tell me what's going on. Nigga, I'm not a mind reader."

103

"I went to see my granny and some bit- some raggedy ass lady with a cheap ass wig said she is my granny's daughter," I paused.

"Ok so you got an aunt." He shrugged.

I slammed my fist on the slate. "*No!*" I shouted then lowered my tone. "No, she is saying she's my granny's only child and don't know who the fuck I am. I tried asking my granny but she so out of it she can't even give me a solid answer. Man, who am I? Why me? Why would she lie to me?"

I was losing it by the second the more I talked about it. Chevy's face held a bit of confusion just as I have been feeling since finding out. "That's yo granny my nigga. It doesn't matter what anybody says or who comes and goes. You know the person that's been raising you all these years. So, why let it stress you? What does this lady want? Everybody wants something so what is it she wants?" he said to me.

He ran one hand down his head. "Diamond, think about it. All these years passed, and this lady has never been around until her mother is sick. She wants something. Give me the number and I'll make sure she gets it to go away."

Chevy always found a solution to our problems, but we never had one for his. I wasn't about to let him solve this issue it was one I knew I needed to solve on my own. "Nah, Chev, I'll handle this one. I needed to talk to somebody."

"Sounds like you the one that needs the pussy," he joked but didn't smile.

"I'm seeing a little shorty," I paused. "I'm seeing Navi's sister," I eased out.

His eyes flicked. "Hmm," he said. "Rayana?"

"Yeah, how you know? Nigga don't tell me you fucked with her because I—"

"Nah, we just ran into each other before. Listen, I'm going to tell you like I told Preach. If she is for you then she is for you, but they Daddy. Watch him."

I slowly nodded. "Oh, Blaze N Fire they been on some shit. We took them to the Zoo," I told him. "They're looking for you."

He raised his brow then nodded. "Me huh?" he flicked his nose. "Bet."

"You good though, what can I do for you my nigga you know we got you on the outside," I asked him.

"I'm straight. Zoo over everything," he said. "Aye Diamond. Remember what I said. Go find you some pussy my nigga, calm down and then approach the situation."

I nodded as I hung up the phone.

***

I couldn't wait to see Yana. Not seeing her for the last few days had taken a toll on me. I didn't want her to think for a second, I hadn't thought about her because I have. I had so many emotions going through me I didn't want her to see me in such a vulnerable state. I pulled up to her place. She lived in a small apartment complex. I stepped up to her door gently knocking. The door opened and seeing her was like a breath of fresh air. She didn't smile as she usually did when she saw me.

"What's wrong?"

She wiped the single tear that slid from her face. Here it was I was worried about myself when it was clear she was going through something as well.

"I don't want to put my burdens on you," she whispered.

"Your burdens are mine. I got you, remember?"

She took me by the shirt pulling me inside wrapping her arms around me. The shit felt so good. This feeling was one I'd never felt before not even with Mo. I wrapped my arms around tightly. I liked Yana a lot. When she glanced up at me, I wiped another tear that found it's way out from her eye.

"I'm tapping out," I told her.

"I want you to tap in," she mumbled.

I leaned in kissing her. Nigga saw sparks fly as we embraced each other in a passionate tongue battle. I picked her up carrying her to her room. She pulled her lips away from me. "Diamond I've never been with anyone other than Malik and I'm scared."

DIAMOND- LAND

In my eyes, she was basically a virgin. I knew whatever we did at this point Rayana, and I would forever be a part of each other, and I was ok with that. I put her down on her feet. Taking her chin into my hand. "I will take it slow. If you want me to stop, I will."

A smile eased on her face. "I want to go to Diamond Land," she said as she pulled me in for another kiss.

I moved away removing my shirt from my body. Yana had my back without asking. She made sure to cater to my feelings, and I was going to do the same for her. If it meant a nigga had to slow stroke her all night I would.

"Turn around," I instructed her.

She did as I asked, I pulled her silk top off then came out the rest of my clothes. I removed the shorts she had on as well. I ran my tongue up the back of one of her legs, up her ass, and up the middle of her back until I reached her neck. "Oo," she moaned.

I reached around gripping her neck from the front, pressing her back against my chest. Tilting her head slightly I let my tongue play with her neck while my other hand played with her pussy. Yana's mouth fell open as she dropped her hips moving with my fingers. Watching her grimacing face was like watching art being made. I went from using one finger to two.

"*Ah!*" she cried.

"Pussy so wet," I groaned in her ear. "The softest shit I've ever felt."

"Diamond something is happening," she whined.

"Let it happen, Yana, you're cumin baby, let that shit happen," I said to her as my thumb circled her clit.

Her head dropped forward and a scream escaped her. I laid her on the bed. I was trying my best to keep neutral but deep inside I wanted to take her all the way there, but I knew she wasn't ready for that side of Diamond yet.

I climbed on top of her. "You sure you want to do this?"

"Yes,"

I slid my dick up and down her slit then entered her slowly. "Oo goddamn," I grunted. "So, fucking tight."

You couldn't tell me she wasn't a virgin the way she felt. A nigga had to get his bearings together, before I nutted faster than I wanted to. I took a deep breath and allowed my hips to move slowly. She took the back of my head bringing my face closer.

"I got you, Diamond."

"I got you too baby."

This moment with her was more than sex to me. It seemed we were both going through something and were able to connect on a deeper level. It was as if I was giving myself to her and it made a nigga feel soft.

Hip up, hip down roll. Hip up, hip down roll.

"Ah, what are you doing to me Diamond?"

Hip up, hip down, roll.

"Taking you to Diamond Land, *fuck!*" I found myself moaning.

She gripped my ass pulling me deeper inside.

Hip up, hip down roll.

I dropped my head. "Damn Yana, shit is like heaven, and I want to stay forever,"

Hip up, hip down roll.

"*Woo shit!*" she yelped.

I was about to cum, but she did something. She wrapped her arm around my neck applying pressure moving me and somehow, I ended up on my back.

"*Fuck!*"

She applied pressure to my chest and went to work fucking my head up.

Roll forward, reverse, roll.

Yana was riding a nigga. "Mm, just like a rollercoaster," she moaned.

Roll forward, reverse, roll. Roll forward, reverse, roll.

Her warm center clung to me. So tight, so wet.

My mouth opened and a long, loud growl escaped me. My hand slid up her thighs to her waist as I helped guide her. *Eyes on me.*

Roll forward, reverse, roll. Roll forward, reverse, roll.

109

I was getting lost the more I stared at her. She was sucking me in.

"Mmm, the best ride ever," she moaned.

Roll forward, reverse, roll. Roll forward, reverse, roll.

"Yana, baby I'm about to cum," I grunted.

Roll forward, reverse, roll. Roll forward, reverse, roll.

This battle I was losing. I'd never had a woman out fuck me. She rode me until I came, and then she followed right after. I was hooked. Yana was mine and there was nothing else to it. We cuddled with each other until she had dosed off.

I lay there thinking about everything, and how, despite our issues beyond these walls we still found a way to enjoy each other. I just hoped she felt comfortable enough to open up to me because I hated to have another Mo situation.

I planted a kiss to her forehead as I dosed off.

When I opened my eyes the sound of my TV blaring caught my attention. *Murder she wrote.* The old drama TV series was playing. I figured Diamond had left, as I was expecting because what man you know has sex with you and stays around? I was at least hoping he would say bye, but he hadn't. I was about to get out of the bed when I heard him singing making me glance up at him. Diamond held my cutting board in his hand with a plate of food and a drink on it.

I giggled. *"What would it take here to make you mine for real? I got a taste and now can't keep off my mind."*

"Ok, light skin Giveon."

He came closer setting the cutting board on the bed. "Really?"

"Shit, you barely had dishes in there. I know you were feeling down, so I wanted to make you smile. You want to talk about it?" he asked.

I did but I didn't. I wanted to talk to Chevy, he was the person I needed help from. Diamond already had to deal with the Gloria issue, and I refused to add more to his plate. I glanced at the TV, "You were watching Murder She Wrote?"

He looked at the TV, "Yeah, I remember my granny would turn this on and a nigga knew it was nap time. I would lie on the couch fake sleeping but watching the shit low-key. The old lady so nosy it's how she caught them niggas."

I could tell the situation with his grandma was really bothering him.

"We will figure it out, Diamond."

He dropped his head. "Shit is crazy. One day things are going good next minute a nigga don't even know his own story."

My phone vibrated pulling us both out our thoughts. I reached over to grab it only to see it was my daddy. I knew by now he was made aware Zaria was missing. Diamond looked at me as I glanced at him and then at my phone. I decided to wait to answer.

"We need to talk about yo Daddy. I need you to know that no matter what happens a nigga is feeling you and I've never felt this way before, but your daddy is shady, and his ass is going down."

I didn't understand. "Diamond what—"

"Something isn't right about him. I know it's your pops and you love him as much as I love my granny, but sometimes the hardest pill to swallow comes from the people you love the most."

I didn't know how I felt about what he said. I grabbed the mimosa he made guzzling it down. He stood up, putting on his shirt. He reached into his pocket pulling out his wallet tossing me his credit card. "I got some shit to handle, go buy yourself some dishes, then something sexy, I like lace and make it orange. Tonight, I'm going to fuck you the Diamond way," he finished as he leaned over the bed kissing me.

When he left, I laid back on the bed. I didn't know whether I was smitten or scared.

***

I told Navi and my Dad I would meet up with them, but first I needed to make a stop. When I arrived at the building, I took a deep breath before going in. I spotted a bunch of familiar faces as I walked over to the front desk. When she glanced up at me, she held a bright smile on her face.

"Rayana, what are you doing here? Navanna is not in today."

I smiled back. "I know. I'm here to see someone else, an inmate."

The confused look sat on her face. I pulled a hundred-dollar bill out of my purse. I knew she would tell Daddy she saw me and right now I didn't need him in my business.

"I came to see June Calloway," I said sliding her the money.

She eyed the money. I could tell she was fighting with herself; she snatched the money so fast I knew I had her in my pocket. She made a call and then nodded at the guard. As I walked to the back a chill went down my spine. The only company I had in the room was the guard stationed at the far end. My anxiety heightened upon hearing the door open. I cleared my throat as Chevy appeared on the other side of the glass. Chevy was so handsome, so serious, and guarded. It almost tickled me because he was damn near Zaria's type. She like men she thinks she could save and the way he was, he would be at the top of her list.

When he saw me, his jaws tightened. I knew I wasn't his favorite person right now, but I needed his help. We picked up the phone at the same time.

"I see you still don't know your place."

"I know I'm not the person you want to see right now, but I think we might be able to help each other."

He ran his hand down the back of his neck, "You can't help me, sweetheart."

"Do you always assume the worst? Have some optimism. What if I can get you out of here?"

"What do you want from me? Ain't nothing in this world free sweetheart so get to the point before I hang up on yo ass."

This nigga was tough as nails. "Listen, I haven't said anything because it's not my secret to tell, but my sister is missing, and I don't know many street niggas but something tells me you can find her."

"How you know she just don't want to be around y'all. Maybe she needed space." He shrugged.

This was possible knowing Zaria, but I knew deep down something wasn't right.

"Chevy, please!" I yelled then quickly looked at the guard.

I stuck my hand in my purse pulling out her picture and slamming it against the window. I noticed his eyes light up a tinge. "This is her. Can you help me or not? If you do not help me, I will tell Diamond."

He dropped his head, "Yeah, I'll help you," he calmly said.

"Good, give me a few hours and you will be out of here."

He raised his head looking at me, "You don't have it in you to tell," he said to me as his eyes never wavered.

"I would I—"

"No, you wouldn't 'cause the nigga you fucking with, you don't want to hurt him. I know you and Diamond have something going on and I'm happy for you both. Next time don't threaten me because I'm not that one, sweetheart. Time is ticking, see you in a few hours," he winked, sat the phone down, got up, and walked to the back.

Well damn! I felt bad for any woman dealing with him. I knew loving him was hard. If only he knew what was on the other side of that wall, he had built around himself maybe just maybe he would live for once or at least fight. I left the building feeling a little better. Now it was time to convince Navi to get him out.

"Zaria, fucking Zaria," Cortez said as he paced around me.

Me running into him sent all types of reminders I didn't need. He was my karma, a living hell, one I couldn't get rid of. I regretted every single time I took him back for dumb shit he did, for allowing him access to my pussy, planting his toxic ass nut inside me. I hated him for stealing from me and even more for putting me in the middle of his debt situation.

I sat in a chair in the abandoned house next door to his. I could tell he had been staying here because he had a small setup in the corner next to the window.

"You got them niggas looking for me," he gritted.

"You got them niggas looking for you!" I spat.

He rushed in my face, "No you! You took that money knowing goddamn well it wasn't yours. You just couldn't keep out of it you had to find a way to meddle in my business," he slapped his hands together, "I just needed more time, and you went off and doubled what I already owed. Here it is you're crying about money, and I told you I needed it. I have daughters that need to eat. I was going to pay you back I just needed you to understand, to hold a nigga down, but you didn't hell, you never did."

This man was out of his goddamn mind. "Nigga that was my fucking money. Money I was using to take care of us. Had you said you needed help maybe I would have helped you, but Cortez you have a problem and it's not me. Let me fucking go!"

"I said *No!*" he roared so loud I thought the house rattled.

He rushed over to the window peeping out paranoid as hell. He then started laughing, "I saw your sisters out here the other day. They call themselves looking for me, dumb bitches."

"Watch your fucking mouth. Cortez when I get out of here, you're dead. I swear. And when did you get some kids? You've never said anything about them, nigga you're full of bullshit."

118

That must have triggered him because he started tossing shit and yelling. "My kids are off limits. They mean a lot to me and whatever I got to do to get back to them I will, so if that means I have to feed you to the wolves, so be it. I'm getting back to Toussiant!"

"Fuck you!"

Slap!

Cortez backhanded me so hard my face swung. He'd never put his hands on me before, but now this nigga had lost his mind. I knew it was only a matter of time before he says fuck it and I was a dead girl.

CHAPTER EIGHT

PREACH

Truth Hurts

My tongue slid up her leg slowly, making sure to tap every nerve. The sound of Pretty's light moans filled my ears. It's been a minute since I've touched her this way and I missed it, I missed her. I couldn't wait for all this to cease so I could have my happily ever after. When I reached her inner thigh, I sent light pecks up until I reached her pussy. "Lord, thank you for this meal, Amen," I said, as my lip wrapped around her clit.

The taste of Pretty's pussy was sweet and extra juicy. I opened her up wide as I dived further in.

"Ah, Prentice, mm," she moaned louder.

I hummed on her clit, making her legs tremble. "Hold them shits up, Pretty, don't make me tell you again," I grumbled.

I took two fingers sticking them inside her as my tongue flicked over her pearl.

"Ah, I'm oh my—"

Smack!

"Don't say it!" I barked.

"*Damn!*" she screamed as her pearl thumped in my mouth.

I slurped her up leaving her panting loudly. I lifted, leaning over top of her glancing in her eyes. "I love you, Pretty," I whispered.

"I love you more."

I stood walking to the bathroom cleaning myself up, when I heard a knock at my door, I poked my head out of the bathroom shooting a look at Pretty. She stood coming into the bathroom, "I need to get cleaned up. I'm supposed to meet with my sister and Daddy," she mumbled.

Just hearing her talk about his washed-up ass pissed me off. I hurried to clean my face, threw some mouthwash in my mouth gargled, spit it out, and walked out of the room to the front door. When I opened the door, I wanted to close it immediately.

"Son," my father said.

"Sup pops," I said as I stepped aside.

He came into the crib but, before I could close the door Simone appeared behind him. *Fuck!* She had her head down as she shuffled her feet in my place behind him. "Oh, lord, please be on my side," I said as I closed the door.

"I won't be long," my father started. "Simone tells me that the young man that was arrested at Church is a close friend of yours, yes?"

I nodded as I cut my eyes at Simone. I was hoping she didn't think what she did gave her brownie points because the shit with her, was dead. She was lucky to be alive right now.

"I saw Mr. Richardson in there. That man, he's not one of the Lord. He is a devil someone put on this earth to destroy."

"Pops get to the point."

I could tell whatever he wanted to say was something that had been sitting on him for a while. I could see the beaded sweat forming on his head. "He and Matthew Calloway were friends. Partners," he paused. "They used to go around to businesses in the neighborhood, threatening to shut some down, or harass peoples' livelihoods for money and votes. He came to me once seeking the congregation's vote, threatening me with some type of tax fraud. What I couldn't understand was why Lonnie was involved. Then it made sense. If Matthew Calloway would have won that election, he would have the goddamn police in his pocket and all he had to do was pay Lonnie under the table."

Now shit was clicking. I glanced behind me to see Pretty peeking out the door. Simone stepped in front of me, "Preach, I'm sorry, and if there is anything I can do to—"

"Excuse me, Pastor, but bitch there is nothing you can do to help him. Prentice is accounted for," Pretty snapped.

My father glanced at her and then at me. "You're dating his daughter?"

"Yes."

My father nodded as he headed to the door, "I-I just wanted to help," he mumbled.

I believed this was my father's way of trying to say sorry when all he had to do was say those words, but it's clear it would never happen, and I've already accepted it. Simone didn't even bother to look at me as she left right behind him. Pretty grabbed her purse before coming over to me. She looked stressed since walking into my house earlier. I wanted to pry but I also wanted her to feel comfortable enough to tell me what was going on with her. I figured it had to do with her father, so I let it be.

"I don't want to talk about it. I have to go, I'm sorry about everything Preach."

I pulled her in giving her a kiss to the side of her face, "Tell his ass goodbye."

She said nothing more as she left my house. It was time to get up with my niggas.

I was able to get Constance to agree to meet me at a small diner. She still hadn't let me go see my granny and I was losing it. I didn't even know if they were taking care of her like they were supposed to. I sipped on the water the waitress brought to the table. I spotted Constance coming inside. I could tell she was nervous. The cheap outfit she wore told me what Chevy was saying seemed to be true. When she saw me, she threw her hand up like I was supposed to wave back.

"Hey Diamond."

"We're not friends, what do you want from me?" I jumped right in.

She patted her dry-ass wig as she turned her nose up.

"Look I'm trying to help you."

She patted her hair again.

"Would you leave that crunchy ass wig alone," I gritted. "The longer you take the longer I'm away from my granny so tell me what the price is because I know it's money you want."

"She's not your grandmother. She's merely an older lady who felt bad for a mixed-breed nigga like you!"

It was taking everything in me not to knock her ass out like the man she looked like. "I'm trying my best not to go ape shit on yo ass, so I'm going to ask again, what do you want?!"

She sighed loudly glaring out of the window. "Momma had always been so big-hearted to everyone but me. I never understood why she took a liking to the broken kids in the neighborhood when she had a broken child sitting in front of her," she said as she ran her hand down that crunchy ass wig again. "I promised once I was old enough, I would leave and never come back. Hell, it wasn't like she was going to miss me anyway. So, the first chance I got I left. I went running so far away I didn't want her to find me if she tried, but it's clear she didn't have to because she found a stray to take care of," she said now looking at me. "I want two hundred and fifty thousand and momma's house."

Her eyes held no sympathy she knew exactly what she wanted. "You're not getting her house," I told her. "I will get you the money, but her house, no, fuck no."

She heckled as her face had now become serious. "My mother has never poured into me like she did you. She owes me that house. My daddy worked day and night to get it, and I want it. So, it's either the money and the house or you will not see her," she said as she stood up.

"If all of what you're saying is true. That I'm a stray and she took me in. We experienced two different people. The love Gloria gave me is one I wish you could feel. If it were me in your shoes, I would worry less about who she took in and more about finding the part of her you're missing. The lady you seem to care nothing about, I care for and if I have to die behind her I will, but your ass is not getting that house," I said to her now standing, and walking away from the table.

I didn't know if I would ever see my granny again, but a nigga was going to do whatever it took to try.

I pulled up to my parents' house. My nerves were starting to get the best of me. Navi's car wasn't here so it meant I had to deal with both my parents by myself. I got out and walked up the driveway to the door. I didn't have to knock because the door swung open to my mother tightly grabbing me in her arms crying her heart out. *They know.* I held onto her tightly. "My baby!" she screamed.

"I know, we're going to find her," I whispered.

She pulled away from me. Her eyes were puffy, runny nose and it looked like she hadn't slept all night. "What if she thinks we're not out there looking for her? What if she's -she is—"

"Maureen, calm down! Zaria is strong always have been, she's a fighter," my father jumped in.

"Navi told you?"

"Navanna didn't say shit. I heard through the department of what happened. I heard she tried breaking into someone's home and Navanna put her on house arrest. I don't know why y'all think I'm dumb. Now my baby girl is missing, and I have to find her."

He was extremely upset. I'd never seen him this way before. He held Zaria's phone in his hand. "Wait, where did you find that?"

He glanced down at his hand. "A block away from her store in the goddamn trash. I bet it was one of the Zoo niggas."

Before I could say another word Navi came through the door. We all looked at her and she stood there like she had been crying. She slowly walked toward my dad.

"I got him out of jail," she mumbled. "You've been lying to all of us."

My mother paused and glanced at him. "What is she talking about Lonnie?"

He said nothing. Navi walked up to him. "You judged someone I love. You wanted him to be the bad person when it's you who's been doing the shit all along. You—"

"You better watch your mouth in my house girl!" my father yelled.

Now everything Diamond was saying began playing in my head.

"A house built on lies. You are a crook, a devil, and a very dishonest man. You locked someone up and you were the cause, Daddy, you were my hero, but a hero no more. I love Preach and he's not going nowhere. But you," Navi nodded. "You might want to fucking pray. Oh, and by the way I quit today. Yana let's go!"

I couldn't believe it. Her and I ran out of the house together. "Navi!" I screamed.

She turned to me, "Chevy told me you came to see him. You could have come to me. We're sisters I'm going to have your back on anything you decide. I may know where she is. Meet me later and we can go find her."

I pulled her in for a hug. "I love you Navi, I swear I do. I asked Chevy to find her. So let him," I whispered in her ear. "You need to go see your man girl," I laughed.

"What's up with you and Diamond?" she asked.

A smile eased on my face. "We're just cool."

"Yeah, well be careful. These men are not just regular men we're dealing with. Oh, and Ray, Malik is dead."

I felt like she punched me in my gut. *Was Diamond responsible for that?* An uneasy feeling settled in my stomach. I didn't know what to think, but I damn sure was about to find out.

DIAMOND- LAND

ZOO-CLAIMER

Upon entering this side of Diamond Land there are a few Zoo Rules.

1. You cannot speak of the Orange Light Special. Everyone deserves to experience it. Please do not share on any platforms of what goes on.
2. Please be sure to always wear your seatbelt and helmet.
3. The use of fruit, explicit language, strong sexual content, sexual use of toys and paddles are used beyond these pages.
4. Remember to embrace and have fun. Now welcome to muhfuckin' Diamond-Land!

YOU CANNOT ENTER IF YOUR'RE THE AGE OF SEVENTEEN OR YOUNGER.

CHAPTER NINE

DIAMOND

Diamond-Land

I'd pulled back up to Yana's. It was later than I anticipated, but I wasn't going the rest of the day without seeing her. I cut the bike off and jogged up to her door. I'd texted her to tell her I was taking her somewhere, so I hope she wasn't on CP time, and she was ready. I knocked on her door waiting for her to answer. When she opened the door a nigga almost nutted because she looked so good.

Her hair was down with loose curls; she wore a brown knitted lace dress with an orange bra and pantie set underneath. "Shit!" I muttered.

A smile filled her face. "Let me grab my coat."

She turned around to walk away but it was more of a slow strut. I noticed it was an orange thong. I was for sure about to spread them fucking hips tonight. She grabbed her coat and purse coming back toward the door. When she saw my bike, she looked at me.

"Cover yourself up, I don't need other niggas seeing what's mine," I told her.

She still hadn't said anything. I led her to my bike, helping her on, and making sure she was fully covered. I placed my lips to her ear giving her a kiss, "You look so fucking good baby," I whispered.

I hopped on the bike taking off. Yana held on to me tightly. *Was I her safe space? Her sense of security.* If not, I wanted to be. I sped through the streets like the night rider. Being with her made me feel like a king. It made me forget the shit I was going through even if it was only for a few hours. I needed her in my life, maybe she had been the missing piece. The void I needed filling. When I pulled up to my destination I parked, then helped her off the bike.

"A hotel?" she asked.

I placed my finger to my lips. We walked in heading straight to the elevator. As soon as the door closed, I pulled the orange eye mask from my pocket. I stepped behind her,

"Remember, I got you. Trust me," I whispered as I placed the mask over her eyes.

I could tell she was nervous, but I was hoping to change all of that tonight. Once the elevator dinged. I got off first taking her hand and leading her down the hall until we reached the penthouse door.

"Tonight, I want to be nasty. I want to show you what Diamond Land is really like. Before we walk through this door, I need to hear you say you trust me," I said to her.

"I trust you, Diamond."

If a nigga could have run down the hall and kicked his feet, I would have. I opened the door leading her inside. I removed her purse from her hand and then the coat from her body. She went to take the mask off, but I stopped her. "Not until I say you can," I told her.

"I smell candles, flowers, and citrus," she said.

She was right but I was about to activate every sense she had.

"Hold your arms up," I instructed her.

She did, I slid the knitted dress off her. I stood back just to take her in. Rayana, to me, was perfection. I got down on my knees crawling toward her. I removed her heels taking each one of her toes into my mouth. "Oo," she moaned.

My tongue slid up her leg snakelike. Until I reached her thong. I used my teeth to pull them down slowly. The smell of her sweet pussy invaded my nose making my eyes roll to the back of my head. Once those were off I stood unlatching her bra. I took one of her nipples in my mouth. "Oh shit!" she yelped.

I sucked on the muhfucka like I had missed a meal. From her nipples, my tongue tapped dance gently on her collarbone to her neck then the side of her face. "*Ssss,*" she hissed.

"I want to tongue fuck this pussy," I said as my finger slid up and down her slit. "I want to fuck you so good, Yana the thought of another nigga is nonexistent."

"Mmm, *ah!*" she moaned.

"Diamond likes to fuck, baby," I said as my lips grazed hers. "I want you to watch everything I do to you. The word no doesn't exist here. So, I'm going to ask you one more time before I take this off, do you want to go to Diamond Land?"

"I-I-I, fuck!" she screamed. "*Yes!*"

I removed the mask from her eyes. She looked at me and then around the room. "Diamond what the hell."

"Aht, ah. Over there," I pointed.

She went to move, "Slow strut, I want to see that ass in slow motion."

Yana looked at me and then nodded. She slowly strutted to the velvet orange couch. Each ass cheek bounced one after the next. When she sat, I opened my two fingers in a V shape, "Spread them wide!" I barked.

When she opened her legs, I came with another set of instructions, "Play with your pussy."

"Diamond I—"

"Play with it, now!"

She eased her fingers to her center and stroked herself slowly. "Yeah, just like that baby," I growled.

I got on my knees crawling her way. Yana's eyes lowered as she took me in. "Keep going baby," I told her.

Closer.

I grabbed a piece of orange dipping it into the jar of honey. I placed one end of it in my mouth as I continued to get closer to her.

Closer.

Yana was working her fingers as her head had now fell back. When I reached her, I pulled the orange from my mouth. "Don't fucking stop," I told her.

I took the honey-covered orange rubbing it on her clit as she stroked herself. I could see she tried scooting back, but I used my hand to grip her thigh. I moved her fingers sticking the orange inside her, my tongue tapped on her clit while she gripped the side of the couch.

"Oh my God, eeehhh," she growled.

I rubbed my nose all in it, taking my tongue scooping the orange out, and sliding it back in. Her legs clinched; clit thumped. She gripped my head pushing my face further as her hips moved back and forth.

"*Ahhh!*"

I tongue fucked her sliding the orange slice in and out of her like a pro. Just like that Yana came and came hard. I took the orange slice in my mouth kissing her and feeding it to her. She ate that shit right up. Helping her off the couch I led her outside, onto the balcony. The city lights and cars were our audience. I came out of my clothes. When she saw me grab the vibrator she hesitated.

"You can't be scary fucking with me, Yana."

I moved her over to the clear glass rail guard. Her back facing me, I strapped each leg so she couldn't move. I picked up my paddle and her eyes widened. "You're my good girl, right?"

"Diamond what—"

Smack!

"That's not what I asked."

"Diamond what the—"

Smack!

"Bad girl! I said are you my good girl?"

She said nothing. *Smack!*

Her head dropped forward overlooking the passing cars. "*Yes!*"

"Diamond is forever baby!"

Smack!

"Say it!"

Smack!

"Diamond, baby you are forever," she whined.

"Good girl, welcome to the fucking Zoo! Now let's fuck!"

I came up behind her stroking my dick between her legs. I snatched her neck to the side digging my teeth into it, as I entered her. "Goddamn!" she cried.

Up then down, hips side to side.

"Good girl's pussy feels so fucking good," I growled.

Up then down, hips side to side.

"Pussy only you can get," she mumbled.

Up then down, hips side to side.

"Pussy so fucking wet," I moaned rubbing my nose against the side of her face.

Yana reached her hand back bringing my face closer. Sticking her tongue in my mouth and kissing a nigga so nasty.

Up then down, hips side to side.

"I want you to fall in love with a nigga. Fuck on this dick Yana, please."

Up then down, hips side to side.

I turned the vibrator on and reached around placing it on her clit.

Up then down, hips side to side.

"Ah, Diamond wha-what the fuck are you doing to me?"

"Baby I'm tapping in. Can't no nigga fuck you like me. I am your nigga. You're a Zoo baby now."

Her hips rocked; her legs shook. She was cumin' and so was I. Her pussy was so good a nigga could cry.

"Diamond I'm about to—"

"Me too baby,"

"Ah, shit!" we said in unison.

Once we were done. We showered together before lying in the bed. She lay on my chest while I stroked her back. "Did you kill Malik?" she whispered.

"That nigga had to go. I would never lie to you. I did."

"Diamond I could have handled him myself."

"I'm your protector let me worry about shit like that."

She said nothing more. We had both dosed off together.

I felt hands gliding up my leg. When I caught a glimpse. Cortez was in front of me. "If you don't get your nasty ass hands off of me," I gritted.

"You're so soft. I haven't felt that pussy in months," he whispered.

Cortez and I hadn't slept together in a while, and for him to think I wanted to throw this ass in a circle for him was beyond me. I was completely turned off and tied the fuck up. I hadn't showered in days; I was hungry as fuck and sleep was minimal. At this point, I felt like nobody was coming for me.

The longer I was stuck here with him the more I knew time was fucking ticking. Cortez stood undoing his pants. He pulled his dick out standing in my face. The smell that came from him made me gag.

"I just want you to suck on the head a little. A nigga needs something."

I gagged, then gagged again. "Cortez, please. I'm not putting that shit in my mouth. You stink!"

Slap!

Another slap to my face. He squeezed my face with one hand and gripped his dick with the other. The closer it got to my mouth. I gagged but tried not to because it would leave my mouth open. Gagged. *Closer.* Gagged. *Closer.*

The sound of a woman's screams stopped him. He quickly pulled his pants up rushing to the window. "Fuck, your fucking sister!" he snapped.

My sister? "*Help! Help!*" I screamed.

Cortez rushed over to me putting his hand over my mouth. I bit down on that bitch. "Help! I'm over here!" I screamed again.

"I said shut the fuck up!"

Everything went black.

"Please, it was just a misunderstanding," Mr. Richardson cried, while hanging from the ceiling.

"*Please, please, please,*" Diamond song.

I walked circles around him. "Did you pray?" I asked.

His body rocked back and forth as fear began strangling him.

"I-I was just trying to protect my daughter."

"You were just trying to do shit! This is bigger than your daughters," I said to him.

He glanced at me curiously. "That's right," I pointed to Diamond. "He too is seeing one of your daughters, so you get a two-for-one fucking deal!" I barked.

Diamond swiveled his head from side to side. "All in it," he giggled.

"Fuck you!"

Clap! Clap! Clap!

"No nigga, fuck you!" the sound of Chevy's voice made Diamond, and I looked back.

Foe and Zu were right behind him. A smile eased on my face. *Fucking Pretty, she really loved a nigga.*

Zu began howling.

"One two, the Zoo Boyz coming for you," Foe started.

I clapped, taunting him. "Three, four, your daughters better lock their doors," I said.

"Five, six, we came to shake up shit!" Diamond sung.

Clap!

"Seven, eight, better come at us straight." Zu howled.

"Nine, ten, can you see us coming," we said in unison.

Chevy wasted no time sending a blow to Mr. Richardson's stomach.

"See, when I saw you in church that day, I knew you looked familiar. You were the coon ass nigga that helped the wonder bread man I called Pops."

Whap!

143

Another blow. He flicked his nose as he came out of his jacket. "I'm not a talking man. However, I have some shit to say!" Chevy jumped up on the table slicing the rope and sending Mr. Richardson slamming down on the concrete busting his mouth open.

"Y'all stripped a young nigga of something. My fucking pride!"

Stomp!

"Integrity!"

Stomp!

"I-I was a different person back then. I have a different side now," Mr. Richardson slurred.

Chevy glanced at me, "This nigga got ten seconds if you need to say something you better do it."

I kneeled lifting his face, "I will take care of her. She doesn't have to worry about nothing. I hope you told her you loved her because if not, too bad. However, the love I will pour into her you won't even matter," I said now standing. "Heavenly Father!" I yelled.

Chevy ran up and drew his arms back with a machete in it. "You said you have two sides. Well, let me slice yo ass in half to see which one I like better!"

He came down splitting Mr. Richardson's head right in two. "*Woo shit!* Come on Bruce Chev'roy," Foe laughed.

"Welcome back my nigga," Diamond stepped up to him.

"Yeah, welcome back!" I said.

We circled around him with no words. Chevy was a true fucking king; one we all loved and would ride for. "Hail to the muhfuckin' king!" Foe yelled.

"Hail to the muhfuckin' king!" we all said.

"Blaze N Fire, up next," Chevy said looking at us all. "Navi and Rayana's sister is missing, and I need to find her. The only thing I can think of is them niggas because they lost that race."

Diamond and I glanced at each other. Navi said nothing about it to me.

"Did you know?" Diamond asked.

"Nah," I replied.

Why wouldn't she tell me something like this?

"We don't have time for brain games. Nigga let's ride!" Chevy yelled.

Normally I would pray when one was dead, but that nigga wasn't getting my good prayer. Foe called up the clean-up crew and we left.

I couldn't wait to get to Navi because I didn't want her to feel like she was going through this alone.

Navi was on a rampage since the day at our parents' house. It was like whatever triggered her, triggered me. We pulled up to Cortez's house jumping out and rushing to the door. I didn't even run back this time I just kicked the door in. The same girl was there with two of her friends. "Bitch where is my sister?!" Navi yelled.

One of her friends jumped up, "Who the fuck are you talking to?"

I snapped. "Not you bitch!"

Whap!

It was three on two, but we didn't care. Navi and I were working them hoes. We were brawling so bad we ended up outside. Navi had the girl by her hair dragging her down the porch as she screamed.

"You fucking on that nigga, bitch," *Whap!* "Where is my sister!" *Whap!*

I thought I heard help, but I couldn't tell because the girl Navi was fighting was screaming so loud. We fought until the neighbors ran up pulling us off. "Tell that bitch nigga Cortez he dead and I will be back every fucking day until he shows up!" Navi screamed.

Once we were in the car Navi screamed at the top of her lungs and then started crying. The stress that was weighing on her was heavy. "Navi, calm down we will find her," I said trying to stay calm.

"It's my fault," she cried.

"It's not your fault. We're going to find her. Chevy will find her," I told her.

I hoped he found her because if anything happened to Zaria I would lose my mind. Navi sat back in the seat crying silently as she gazed out of the window. I wiped the tears that escaped my eyes as I drove off. I needed to get my shit together because I still had to go to work. I dropped Navi off at home, changed my clothes, and headed to work.

I needed Diamond. I needed a form of peace, and he had been the only form of peace I had. Not only could I talk to him, but the way he opened my body up I needed it again. When I got to work, I got myself together. The first place I went to was to Gloria's room. I wanted to check on her make sure she was ok. I noticed her daughter was not in the room when I went in, instead it was Mo.

When she saw me, she jumped up. "Sorry I was just checking on her," she mumbled.

I wanted to talk to her. I wanted to share with her that Diamond was mine and that she needed to stay away. "Sit down," I told her as I closed the door.

I glanced at Gloria who was asleep. "Why are you here?" I asked.

"I said to check on her!" she snapped.

"Why?" I asked again. "Is it that you were hoping Diamond showed up? Huh? Why is it that you are always around him? Popping the fuck up everywhere?"

She rolled her eyes. "Says the person who claimed if the dick makes you act like that you don't need it. He served it to you as well I see," she smirked.

This was true. Diamond definitely had the type of dick that would make you lose your morals and mind. Mo stood coming in my face. "Diamond Blanco belongs to me. Whatever taste you got will be your last," she hissed.

"I fought bitches today I would hate to put this work on you, again. Diamond Blanco, that dick is mine. He doesn't want you and for some reason you're finding it hard to accept. So let me put it to you this way, Mo," I paused now moving closer to her. "Your pass has been revoked. You no longer have access. If I catch you around, these hands would be the least of your worries. Ms. Gloria, she will be fine, she doesn't need you around. Go mend that broken heart, but mend that shit somewhere else because Diamond-Land is closed."

I must have struck a nerve because the look in her eyes softened. She gripped her purse brushing past me before leaving the room.

"You sure told her," Gloria whispered giving a dry laugh.

I took a deep breath. "Hey Gloria, how are you feeling?" I asked.

"Where is Chew?"

"He's um home. Ms. Gloria, why didn't you tell Diamond he wasn't related to you?" I asked.

I wanted answers for him, something I could tell him that would make him feel at ease. She looked at me and then out of the window. "Chew will be alright. Granny made sure of it." Is all she said.

I felt so bad, but I was hoping he got some answers. If she wouldn't talk to me, I knew who she would talk to. My next

move would be risking my job, but for Diamond it was worth
it.

Niggas was out all night looking for Blaze N Fire and found not a single fucking soul. We knew they had to be hiding. Chevy pressed paused on looking for them sending us all home. I'm sure the nigga wanted to sleep in his bed being he'd come right from county jumping into action.

I was worn out. I lay across my couch watching Murder She Wrote. The more I was away from my granny the more depressed I'd become. When I was around my niggas, I was trying to play it cool but in the back of my mind, she was all I could think about. I had so many questions for her. I picked up

151

my phone to see if Constance had called. The bitch was taking forever to tell me if she wanted the money. I knew she wanted that house, but I went through a lot to keep it for my granny, and I wasn't about to allow her to have it.

There was a light tap on my door. I got up from the couch answering it.

"Hey baby," Yana smiled.

I was happy she slid through because a nigga could really use the company before I got into my own head. I gave her a partial smile as she leaned in to kiss me. Every time our lips touched each other it was like a piece of heaven.

"I got a surprise for you?"

I nodded. "What kind of surprise? I hope it has to do with that wet puss—"

"Granny!"

Yana pulled her in front of me. Something was happening to me. I was feeling emotional. Tears welled in my eyes as my granny glanced up at me and smiled. She placed her hand to the side of my face, "Chew, Chew," she said barely above a whisper.

I took her by her hand leading her to the couch. When she sat, I turned toward Yana. "How?"

"Don't worry about it. I knew you missed her, and I just wanted to make you happy Diamond. I got you."

What Rayana had done really placed her at the top of my list. She cared enough to bring the one person I needed to me. I'm not sure how she pulled it off, but the point is she made it happen. There was nothing I wouldn't do for her. I felt a tear trickle down my cheek. Yana use her thumb to wipe it away.

"Big ass baby," she giggled.

"Your baby. Thank you," I told her. "We're going to find your sister baby I promise."

This time when she looked at me, I could tell she didn't want me to know, but I was her protector, her nigga it was my job. "Diamond, I didn't want you to have to worry about it, but thank you," she whispered.

I glanced back at my granny and then at her. "Look, I have some errands to run. I will leave her with you for a few hours and come back. Diamond we really have something to talk about," she said leaving the house.

I went to sit on my granny's side as we watched back-to-back episodes of Murder She Wrote. I laid my head on her lap while we talked about the show. For the first time in a long time, I was scared to ask but I needed to know.

"Why didn't you tell me the truth," I asked her.

She patted my head then stopped. "Chew, I want to tell you a story."

"Granny please with the stories just tell me!" I snapped.

Before she could say something there was a knock at my door. "Who the fuck is it!" I snapped jumping up.

I went to the door swinging it open. "Diamond Blanco, we are here to get Gloria Gaylord. She was taken away from the hospital without permission. Is she here?" a lady in a suit asked.

"Man, don't come here with that bullshit. How you get my address. It's not the address I have on record."

"Sir, we need to know if—"

"Chew, who's that?" my granny asked.

The people barged into my house, and I lost my goddamn mind. I began tussling with the officers behind the lady. "Get yo fucking hands off me. She's not going no fucking where!" I hollered.

Constance stepped inside with her arms crossed, but that's not what got me. Monette came in behind her. "Bitch! You sorry ass, bitch!"

The officers held me down as they escorted my granny out. She turned to my crying; my fucking granny was crying. "Chew I'm sorry. Let him go!"

The lady grabbed her arm a little t hard for me.

Whap! Whap!

I hit the officer.

"Momma, calm down!" Constance yelled at her.

"I'm sorry Diamond," Mo said.

"Sorry, bitch you gone be sorry, fuck you!"

My granny clenched her arm. Something was happening. Her knees buckled. "Diamond," she gasped.

They tried to hold her up. My eyes widened; my breathing became heavy. My eyes bounced all over. I rushed over to her on my knees holding her in my arms. The tears poured out of me because God was taking her back. He wasn't supposed to do it this way. Had I been so selfish worried about the wrong thing that God decided to take her. I glanced down at her sweet face.

"*Granny!*" I called out to her.

It sounded like she was wheezing, "Do something!" I screamed.

She looked at me and smiled. Then her eyes went up staring off into the ceiling. "*No, no, no, no,*" I cried.

I rocked her back and forth until they'd come to carry her out. Everyone left my house as I sat there on the floor. I couldn't wrap my mind around what happened.

"Diamond!" I heard Rayana call my name, but I couldn't move.

Rayana squatted in front of me. "Diamond, what happened?"

My eyes slowly raised to her. This was her fault. She took her from the hospital causing all the commotion and my granny couldn't take it.

"This is your fault. She's dead because of you!" I shouted. "Get the fuck out!"

"Wait, Diamond I-I—"

"Get the fuck out!" I practically growled at her.

Her head flew back, she stood, turning to leave. I slammed the door behind her. I didn't want to be, but a nigga was broken.

I hadn't slept all night after Diamond kicked me out of his house. I thought what I was doing was helping him. I didn't know things would happen the way they did. As much as I wanted to curl up in my bed and cry the day away, I still had problems on my end to deal with. Which was my sister.

I pulled up to Chevy's. I got out of the car, going up to his door. I knocked a few times and waited. The door swung open, and it was a girl. I'd seen her before at Diamond's party.

"Is Chevy home?"

She kept a neutral face so I couldn't tell if she wanted to say something smart or not, but I hoped she didn't because I wasn't in the mood to fight a bitch today. She stepped back letting me inside.

"Chev!" she called out.

Moments later he appeared from the back. "Again, another place you don't know."

The girl looked at me then at him. "Don't worry Harvey, she's harmless. What can I do for you?"

"You want to talk about it in front of her?"

"You need to worry less about her and more about me. Again, Rayana what can I do for you?"

His attitude was getting on my fucking nerves. "You're supposed to be looking for my sister!" I yelled.

I didn't mean to, but I was under so much stress. "First, stop yelling in my fucking house. My plants can hear that shit. Second, I am," he said stepping closer. "Why didn't you tell Diamond what was going on? Why me?"

"Diamond was dealing with Gloria and I—"

"What you mean was?"

Observant. I dropped my head. *Shit!* "She passed away yesterday," I mumbled.

Harvey gasped. "Chev, we got to go see him!"

He glanced at her and then back at me. "Fuck you mean she passed. Where is he?"

158

"I-I don't know because he kicked me out of his house," I broke down. "I tried helping by bringing his grandmother to him and she died!" I wailed.

I felt so bad. It was eating away at me. "Now he doesn't want to see me," I sobbed.

Harvey came over embracing me. "He's just hurting."

"Fuck!" he shouted. "I'm going to go check on him. Harvey make sure she gets home and get whatever info you can about her sister, hit me," he said.

Chevy grabbed his keys leaving the house. Harvey walked me over to the couch. "You have to calm down. It wasn't your fault. These Zoo Boyz aren't easy to deal with," she said.

"How do you deal with Chevy; how do you love him?"

She laughed. "Chevy and I are like brother and sister. We grew up together, but I understand because I too deal with one of them," she paused then cleared her throat. "They all have been through things it is what makes them so close. Loving them is not easy hell, them loving us isn't easy. So, it's either you're going to stick beside them or walk away. Diamond, is just hurting."

I sniffled. "I don't know what to do."

She squeezed me, "He will come around give him time. You a Zoo baby now. Just remember, we only fuck with the Zoo," she smiled.

Harvey and I sat in Chevy's place talking for hours. I told her all about Zaria, we sat and went back and forth about different places we could look. She was easy to talk to and I liked that. She sent Chevy a text. While we waited, we continued to talk. Although our conversation was good. I couldn't stop thinking about Zaria.

I missed my sister and couldn't wait to see her, hopefully alive.

I sat in the church kneeling before the pulpit. I prayed and asked God for guidance on my next move. I told Pretty to meet me here because there were things we needed to talk about, and I wanted to do it before God. I didn't want any lies or holding back. We were still in the midst of God's storm I could feel it.

I heard the doors to the church open as her heels clicked on the floor. "Come pray with me," I told her without looking.

I could smell her perfume. She came up to the pulpit kneeling along with me. I took her hand into mine. "Bow your head," I said.

I opened my eyes to see her bowing with her eyes closed. "Heavenly Father, I asked that you give us strength. Strength for what's to come. Strength to Pretty for she will need healing. Lord, God, I asked that you forgive me for the things I've done and help guide me in the right direction. You said, God, he who findeth a wife findeth a good thing. So, I'm asking you to bless us and the union we're going to step into. Pretty, I told you that you were going to be my wife. I've prayed countless hours about it and received the same message each time. I'm not the perfect man, but I'm your man. I promise I will protect you; I will support you, and I will love you until God decides to take my last breath," I paused letting go of her hand. "Open your eyes."

When she looked at me her eyes watered. Her lips trembled.

"Navanna Pretty Richardson, will you do me the honor of being my wife. Will you marry me?"

A light sob fell from her lips, as the tears tickled down her cheeks. It made me a bit emotional, but I knew what I was doing was the right thing. I wanted to ask her this way, so she knew the man she was choosing to spend the rest of her life with was not only sincere, but also placed everything on the table in front of God.

"Yes, yes, and yes again," she smiled.

I slid the ring on her finger kissing her. She wrapped her arms around me pulling me in close. "About your father," I whispered.

"Preach don't. Let me believe he ran off and decided to leave his family because he couldn't bear what he did, please."

She knew the truth and that's all that mattered. "I love you Prentice," she mumbled.

"Not as much as I love you."

We both stood and my father stood there smiling. "I'm so proud of you son and I'm so sorry," he broke down.

I rushed up to him embracing him in a hug I hadn't had since I was a young boy. "I love you son," he cried.

"I love you too pops."

I pulled away going back over to Pretty. My phone vibrated and it was a text from Chevy saying I needed to get to Diamond's his grandmother passed. I kissed Pretty telling her I would see her later. Rushing out of the church. My nigga needed me, and I was going to be there.

CHAPTER
THIRTEEN

DIAMOND
Brotherhood Over Everything

I'd found myself drinking an entire bottle of cognac. I couldn't wrap my mind around the fact my granny had lied to me all these years and now she was gone. She left this earth without me. I felt empty, numb, and confused. Rayana's, intentions were pure, but she should have just left well enough alone. I was angry at Mo for even giving my fucking address. I was mad at Constance for trying to blackmail me. One bitch after the next betrayed me. It was the main reason I refused to give my heart away.

"Bitches!"

I sat in the empty lounge, glancing around. I hit play on the remote to allow the music to fill the lounge. I placed the blunt to my lips, inhaling and exhaling like I would never smoke again. I held the bottle in the air as I bounced to the music.

"Granny you left me," I said aloud.

Inhale, exhale. Head bounce. Head bounce.

"*Fuck!*"

Inhale, exhale. Head bounce. Head bounce.

I spun in a circle, bouncing to the music. *Bottle to my lips. Then blunt.* Every woman that I had ever crossed paths with invaded my brain. *Keisha, Layana, Tamika, Raquel, Kitty, Redd, Michelle, Lia, Mo, Rayana.*

I saw the door to my lounge open and in walks Mo. She stood there looking good as hell. It could have been that I was high and drunk, but I needed to feel something. She slowly eased my way. I stood there now placing the bottle to my lips, taking a long guzzle. I wiped my mouth with the back of my hand as she was now standing in front of me. I glanced down at her.

"Dia—"

"Shh," I said to her. "Turn around and bend over," I instructed her.

My head began spinning. I took another guzzle from the bottle, tossing it on the floor. I watched Mo as she turned, poking her ass out. She glanced at me and smiled. I ran my hand over her ass, smacking it. She swiveled left to right. I felt my phone vibrating in my pocket but ignored it. I rubbed up and down her body. My hand eased up to her head as I took a grip on her fancy ass lace. I yanked her head back.

I rocked my hips from side to side on her ass. I used my free hand rolling her dress up. "This all you want. Dick!" I barked.

I pulled her head back further. "Diamond, you're hurting me," she whined.

"You hurt me Mo, why would you send those people to my house? Huh!" I shouted.

I pulled at her panties until I ripped them off. I let go of her hair now gripping both sides of her waist. "Mo you know you really fucked up. I warned you so many times and you just had to keep on," I told her.

I was seething. My hands moved up slowly, I heard her moan. When my hands reached her neck, I squeezed. *Tighter.* "I hate you Mo!" *Tighter.* "You are a fucking problem!" *Tighter.* "I don't call women bitches, but you Mo, you're a fucking bitch!" *Tighter.*

She clawed at my hands, but I wouldn't let up. I shook her by her neck. "Fuck you, Monette!"

I felt a pair of hands on my arms, "Yo Diamond nigga chill!" Foe said.

"Fuck off me!" I said yanking away rushing back to Mo.

166

DIAMOND- LAND

"Zu nigga, get yo big ass over here and help me nigga, he strong as fuck," Foe said to Zu.

"It's her fault!" I shouted as they dragged me backward.

"Fuck you Mo, fuck you. A nigga wished he never met you, you a sleazy ass broad."

Chevy appeared stepping in front of her. "I'm going to give you this. Your best bet would be to leave and never come back. Monette, if I see you, I will kill you," he calmly said to her.

She took whatever it was rushing out of the lounge. Chevy came over to me, "You, ok?"

I dropped to my knees breaking down. I tried getting myself together, but I couldn't. I cried. I was sobbing like a baby.

"We here for you, my nigga. Let that shit out," Zu said to me rubbing my back.

"She was all I had."

"God will see you through my nigga. He will. You want to pray about it?" I heard Preach.

They all came in around me embracing me in a hug. These niggas were my brothers, niggas I'll do whatever for and in this moment proved that Zoo was everything. We were more than niggas who killed and rode bikes. We were men who went through shit together we were a brotherhood.

"We love you my nigga," Foe said.

The sound of motorcycles zooming by caught Chevy's attention. He rushed out of the lounge door.

"Aye Preach, let's ride."

"Nah, we all riding," I said to him.

We all rushed out of the building. I wiped my eyes, locked up, and hopped on my bike. We all took off down the street. "You sure you good, Diamond?"

"I need this right now, ride nigga stop talking to me, Foe."

Left lane, right lane, dip low, swerve. We hit that corner so smooth.

"Blaze N Fire, you think they got her?" Zu said.

"Only one way to find out!" Chevy shouted as he took off doing a wheely.

"That boy Chev cold, ooo wee!" Preach laughed. "I asked her to be my fucking wife, and she said yes!"

"One time for the nigga Preach!" I shouted.

All five of us popped a wheely at the same time. The orange lights from our bikes lit up the street. "Congratulations my nigga!" Chevy said to him.

"Yeah, what that nigga said," Foe jumped in.

We had now slowed down halting at the end of the block. We saw the niggas stop on a residential street. "How are we going to go down this block without them knowing were behind them?" Zu asked.

"Who gives a fuck!" Chevy said taking off down the block.

DIAMOND- LAND

I knew it was time to get ready because once Chev was on go, it was all gas no fucking brakes.

I was giving up, surrendering to whatever it was Cortez wanted. My body was weak as hell, my face was sore from all the times he'd slapped me around. I could no longer feel my arms because they had been tied up for so long. Nobody was looking for me, I was tired.

My head fell forward rolling from side to side. "Cortez," I barely got out.

I didn't hear movement. "Cortez!" I shouted.

"Shut the fuck up!" he snapped.

My eyes shifted his way. He was peeking out the window again. "I will give you the money, just let me go please," I whined.

He quickly crawled my way, "Shut up. They out there looking for me."

Someone is outside? This is the last chance I have. I licked my lips and took in a deep breath, I rumbled up the loudest help I could. "*Help!*"

Cortez rushed over to me, his eyes widening while gritting his teeth. "Didn't I tell—"

Someone kicked the door in, and Cortez scrambled to get away. My eyes focused on the men coming in and it was Blaze N Fire. I heard a lot of tussling but couldn't make out what was going on. That's when someone stepped in front of me, smiling. He leaned over untying my hands and throwing me over his shoulder. "Thought you got away, didn't you? You're a sneaky little bitch."

"Only bitch I see is one who's about to be eating bullets!" I heard a familiar voice.

My eyes fluttered as more men came through the door. It was Mystery Man. *He found me!*

"I warned yo ass. Put her down, she's too pretty to have your fucked up thoughts on her," he gritted.

Suddenly my body slammed against the floor knocking the wind out of me. I tried getting up, but I was too weak. When I glanced up Mystery Man had the gun to the back of the man's head.

"Supa nigga to the rescue," the man said to him as he slowly turned around.

Whap!

He hit him with the butt of the gun in his nose, "The nigga that's going to be whooping yo ass supa crazy."

I glanced around and it was Blaze N Fire against the Zoo Boyz. It was so much shit going on. I was looking for Cortez hoping he was getting his ass whooped but I didn't see him. Mystery Man used his foot to close the door.

"Normally I would take y'all corny ass niggas to the Zoo, but y'all won't make it that far," Mystery Man said.

"Bitch nigga sit the fuck down!" One of the Zoo Boyz gritted hitting a guy in the head with the butt of his gun.

By the time I got up, three men were sitting side by side with the Zoo Boyz holding guns to their heads. My eyes searched out until it landed on the back door. Cortez had gotten away. *Shit!*

Mystery Man looked at me, "Sorry sweetheart, you're about to witness a homicide. Cause we not leaving this muhfucka until all these niggas eating bullets."

Preach came over to me, "You, ok?"

I nodded.

"Man, Lucas gone fuck y'all up!" someone from Blaze N Fire shouted.

"Any, many, miny, Moe one of you niggas got to go," one of the Zoo Boyz guns bounced on the guys on the floor.

Blaow!

The guy's body fell backwards.

"One down three bitches to go!" Diamond yelled.

"So, you going to kill us?" the guy that had picked me up said.

"Nah, you niggas were so thirsty to run up in here to snatch her up so let me quench that thirst for you, *next!*" Mystery Man shouted.

Preach looked at me, "Close your eyes," he whispered.

"Heavenly Father!" I heard Preach shout.

"*Swing Lo, Sweet chariot.*" Diamond song.

"I hope y'all prayed today!" Preach yelled.

These niggas were crazy as hell. Zoo Boyz was very fitting. It was like they were entertaining you before dying.

"Just shoot his ass and stop playing," one of them said.

"You know what, fuck it!"

Bloaw! Blaow! Blaow!

"Damn Foe, you stay trigga happy," Diamond said to him.

"Happy on the fucking trigga," he smiled.

"Yo Chev, you want us to get her out of here?" The bigger one asked.

Chev? The way he stared at me was just like my dream. I couldn't move, all I could do was stare back. His eyes darkened, his jaws tightened but he never took his eyes off me. *I got you.* He mouthed.

"Nah, y'all step out for a second," he told the guys as his eyes never wavered.

They did exactly what he asked.

"Come here," he said to me.

I slowly stood easing up to him. He took his gun putting it in my hand. He stood behind me pressing his body to my back making me shudder. I knew it was odd, but he was turning me on. He leaned forward placing his lips to my ear. "I'm Chevy and you are?" he whispered.

The tingle that went through me was electrifying, "Za-Zaria," I mumbled.

"Nice to meet you, Zaria. I want you to shoot his bitch ass," his raspy voice gritted.

He slowly placed his hands on top of mine, moving his body closer to mine. *Lips back to my ear.* "I want you to hold this muhfuckin' gun like you're holding dick. Grip it tight, you control it don't let it control you and when it feels good squeeze that fucking trigger," he growled.

My pussy thumped. I took in a deep breath exhaling slowly. He placed his hand around my waist pulling me closer to him.

I could feel his thumb slowly stroking my belly. My eyes closed for a mere second.

"Man, what type of freaky shit you on?"

"Shut yo horse mouth ass up! Nigga you dying today."

"I should have smoked yo ass the first chance I got," the guys said to him.

Lips to my ear. "Pull it, pull it, pull it, pull it, pull it," he hummed.

Thumb stroking my belly, lips grazing my ear, belly stroke. lip graze.

"You look good as fuck holding my gun in your hand. Yeah, just like that," Chevy just kept going.

It was like he was fucking me by talking and the more he talked the more my body felt hot, and my pussy thumped. I pulled it.

Bloaw!

"Good girl," he said spinning me around.

I took in a deep breath, exhaling loudly. We had no space between us. Dark as fucking midnight, this man was so fine, so smooth with it, and mysterious. I almost wanted to be lost in his world. He pulled his eyes away disconnecting the trance I was in.

"Now let me get you to your sisters. They sent me to look for you," he winked.

DIAMOND- LAND

My body just went through something I'd never experienced, and he'd just made me kill someone. I didn't know what to think, but right now I needed to get out of here.

When Chevy brought Zaria to us it was like I could breathe again. Seeing her in the shape she was in made my heart ache. We had all decided to stay the night at my place. All three of us sat on the couch wrapped in one blanket watching one of our favorite throwbacks. Sixteen Candles.

Zaria laid her head on my shoulders. While tossing popcorn in her mouth. Navi clearing her throat made us look at her.

"Zaria, how are you feeling? I know a lot has happened."

Zaria lifted her head and shrugged. "I was scared, but honestly, I just wanted to get out of there. I can't believe

177

Cortez put me threw all that and still his ass got away," she said.

"We're going to find his ass, I promise," I jumped in.

"Y'all know this nigga got kids?" she said.

Navi and I gasped. "Oh yeah, he's a fuck nigga!" I shouted. "What man doesn't tell you about his kids."

"I have something to tell y'all," Navi mumbled.

Zaria and I turned our heads toward. "I'm about to be an aunt?" Zaria squealed.

"Uh, no slow your roll," Navi laughed.

She held her hand up and at first, I didn't know what she was doing it for until I saw a big-ass pretty rock sitting on her finger. Zaria and I both jumped up.

"Congrats Navi!"

"Y'all Preach is just," she paused. "He's everything I swear."

I began thinking about Diamond. He and I hadn't talked since he kicked me out of his house. A tinge of jealousy hit me. Navi had found her happily ever after and here I thought Diamond was forever, but I was wrong.

Zaria chimed in, "The Zoo Boyz are fucking crazy for sure, but they have a bond within their circle that's good for them. I can tell," she said, looking at me. "What's up with you and Diamond?"

I didn't want to talk about it. I was ashamed. I lost my job, lost my man and now I was watching my sister in pure excitement. "He and I didn't work out," I muttered.

Tap! Tap!

Navi looked over my shoulder, "Y'all heard that?"

Zaria and I looked back. "No," we said together.

Tap!

I heard it this time. I got up going to my window. When I peered out the window. I saw Diamond and Preach standing there. I raised the window.

"Nigga there she goes hold the fucking radio up!" Diamond said to Preach.

Zaria and Navi ran up behind me leaning all on me. I used my elbow to push them off.

"I want to see too," I heard Zaria giggling.

Preach held up the radio as Diamond started crooning.

"*Try me, try me,*" he sang now closing his eyes. "*Darlin', tell me I need you,*"

"Is this nigga singing again," I heard Zaria.

"Girl shut up and let the man sing," Navi jumped in.

"*Uh, oh, walk with me, talk with me, I want you to stop my heart from cryin' oh, uh oh, walk with me,*"

The sounds of my sisters going back and forth bothered me. I pushed their asses out the way running outside. Diamond was still singing with his eyes closed while Preach had now set the radio down. Meanwhile, I was cheesing like a fucking Cheshire cat.

"Nigga you can stop," Preach tapped his arm but Diamond kept going.

I didn't care I ran up to him wrapping my arms around his neck. He picked me up placing both hands to my face. "A nigga sorry. I-I—"

I kissed him. I kissed him the Diamond way, nasty. He walked me back up the steps into the apartment. My sister's stared at us curiously.

"Y'all can stay, or you can go, but I'm fucking him in that room," I said to them.

Diamond carried me to the back closing the door behind him. I didn't care about nothing in the moment except, him.

Being in Yana's presence made me feel good. I knew I had taken my anger out on her, but I was just so upset. I knew her intentions were genuine but at the time none of that mattered. When I went up to her job to talk to her and they told me she no longer worked there I felt like shit. I spent the last couple of days trying to convince myself that Yana was merely a quick season and us being together couldn't work, but every time I thought about what my world would be like without her in it; I couldn't.

She and I had made a connection bigger than sex. She knew what I needed. She knew how to cater to my feelings and my granny actually fucked with her. I couldn't let her go. I was able to talk Preach into helping me. Shit, I helped him it was an even trade.

When I closed the door behind me, I put her down. She glanced up at me. "I'm so, so sorry Diamond. I really was trying to help and had I known I wouldn't have done it," she explained.

"I know. I miss her something crazy, but it's not your fault and I'm sorry for even blaming you, can you forgive me?"

"If you can forgive me?" she said. "I want to go to Diamond Land," she whispered while removing her clothes.

"You have full access I told you," I smiled.

She backed away until she reached the bed. She was on all fours fully naked. I came out of my clothes walking over to the bed. "No, I want to see your face while I make love to you," I told her.

"Wait, you said you like to fuck."

"Yeah, but right now I want to make love, because," I paused. "A nigga loves you," I said.

I did, I loved her. Rayana had a nigga's heart, and I wasn't ashamed to say it. She trapped me, swooped into my heart, snatching it. I never thought I would be this open for someone like I was with her, but a nigga was open wider than a muhfucka. I slowly climbed on top of her.

Peck to the lips. Another then another. She wrapped her arms around my neck as I entered her. "Mm," I moaned.

This time shit felt different. She was warmer, wetter, tighter. Her pussy wrapped around me, and it felt like love. It spoke to me in a way that had a nigga ready to cry. I dropped my head pressing my forehead to hers.

"Yes, mm, Diamond," she whimpered.

"Fucking heaven, mm," I moaned.

Circle, up then down.

"Ah!" her moan sounded like music.

Circle, up then down.

"Diamond is forever," I grunted.

"Oh my, Diamond you are forever," she cried.

A tear slid from the corner of her eye. I ran my tongue to the side of her face licking it up, "Don't cry baby."

Circle, up then down.

Then a part of me felt choked up. I didn't know what was happening, but something was. Her pussy was bringing a softer side out of me, one that I wasn't expecting. My eyes watered and a tear escaped me. She pulled my face down and did just as I had. She licked it the fuck up.

Circle, up then down.

"I love you, Diamond."

She gripped my neck spinning me and I was on my back. My head fell back, and my mouth opened. *"Fuck!"*

"That's right fuck me baby," she moaned.

Thumb to her pussy, *Circle, circle.*

She squeezed her breasts together while rolling her hips. *Circle, circle.*

One hand to her waist, the other to her neck. Flip. She was now on her back with her legs gripping my waist. Another tear fell from my eyes landing on her lips. A nigga was really in love.

"I'm so in love with you, Yana," I moaned.

I felt the nut brewing up. "I'm about to cum baby,"

"Me, ah, *too!*" she howled.

We had come together. I was happy we had made up and she would be by my side because in the next few days, I had to lay my granny to rest, and I was going to need all the support I could get.

Rayana and I decided to go visit Chevy. I wanted to thank him for not only saving me, but also what he'd done to keep my store open. He had come like a thief in the night into my life and somehow always managed to get me out of some shit. It was only right I showed my gratitude.

When we pulled up to his home I was blown away because I wasn't expecting this. The man lived like a king. His home was big but something about it was peaceful. As we pulled further into the driveway, I saw his bike and that damn caprice that almost hit me. It was the first time we met, and a giggle escaped my lips thinking about it.

"What are you laughing for, you like him don't you?" I heard Rayana.

I quickly turned my head to her. "No, the man just helped me out and I'm thankful."

"Mm hmm. Chevy is kind of your type. He needs someone like you, trust me. He's going through a lot," she said.

What did she mean by that? Rayana parked the car and got out with me behind her. When we walked up to the door she knocked. I anxiously waited for him to open the door. I almost wanted to bust inside wrap my arms around his neck and kiss him. The locks click and my stomach flutter. I let out a light exhale.

When the door open and he stood there I fucking melted. His eyes to mine. His face remained serious, but it was almost as if I could read his mind.

You look beautiful.

Thank you.

"Hey!" Rayana said to him.

He pulled his eyes away looking at her, "How can I help you ladies?"

"You going to let us in or keep us outside?"

Chevy stepped back allowing us inside. I thought the outside was amazing, but the inside my God. It was so fucking peaceful. I spotted the plants and laughed to myself. Then the orange accent wall and chair. This nigga really likes orange.

I glanced back over at him. *Eyes on me.* Something was going on with him, I could tell.

What's wrong?

I'm fine.

"We came to say thank you," Rayana said.

He pulled his eyes away again. *Shit! I wish she shut up.*

I smiled. "Yeah, I wanted to come to you personally to say thank you for saving my life."

He winked. "You saved your own life."

Before I could say another word. Someone knocked at the door. He stepped away toward the door, and when he opened it, a woman wrapped her arms around his neck kissing him. My heart sank. *Fuck!* He was taken. I should have known. The man was pure perfection, and I shouldn't have expected anything less. I tapped Rayana on her arm, "Come on let's go," I whispered.

She followed behind me as we made our way to the door. He glanced at me but this time I didn't allow my eyes to rest on him long enough for us to even communicate. The woman looked at us curiously as we walked by. We got in the car as I took one last look. It seemed like they were arguing but I didn't care.

Chevy was off-limits.

I headed towards Chev's because there was something I wanted to talk to him about. The shit had been sitting on me for months and it was time to ask. As I drove up the hill toward his house, I saw Rayana flying past me. I'd wondered what she came here for. I continued to drive up the hill until I reached his spot. When I saw Lola outside his door, I knew shit was about to pop off.

Chevy didn't like her, and she was almost as bad as Simone and Mo. I quickly hopped out of my car jogging toward them.

"Lola get the fuck off my property! That shit you pulled will get you shot, sweetheart," Chevy told her.

"I've been looking for you and you've been ignoring me. Now what is it going to be huh? Your friend here now I could just tell him!" she screamed.

Tell me? I looked at Chev then at her. I stepped to the side of Lola, "You got to go shorty," I told her.

She snatched away from me as she started talking in Spanish. "Listen!" I shouted. "I don't give a fuck what you talking about, you better leave before the next words coming from your mouth will be calling on Jesus!"

She looked at me then at Chevy.

"Lola, sweetheart," Chevy said placing prayer hands to his lips as he stepped outside of his house closer to her. "This is the last time I'm going to say this. I can promise you, a nigga will kill you. I will cut off that fake ass, send it to your daddy just to show him how much of an ass he has for a daughter if you come back around here!"

"Damn!" I yelled.

Chevy's mouthpiece was one not to play with and most of the time the shit he said he meant. Lola stood there she knew better than to say another word. She slowly eased back and got in her car speeding down the driveway. If she was a man, she would have been long gone. That was the hardest part about what we did because we tried our hardest not to put women down like animals. Chevy stepped back inside his place with me behind him.

He lit a blunt sitting on the couch. I sat in the orange chair adjacent to him. I watched Chevy as he smoked. Something seemed different about him. *Had he lost a little weight? He seemed a little flushed. No is it his eyes?* I couldn't put my finger on it, but it was something.

"What's up Preach?"

"Shit checking on you," I said to him.

"What's the real reason you're here?"

Chevy was smart, the nigga knew everything. He didn't miss a beat. I cleared my throat. "I wanted to ask you something. This trip you want to take, is it really about you going to see your mother or something else?"

He cut his eyes at me as he pulled the blunt from his lips. "It's about my mother, why?"

I leaned back in the chair, "The shit was so random and you leaving the crew still doesn't sit right with me," I explained.

"I'm still here, right? I'm still riding. Y'all niggas have me until I dip. Zu, he and I still have some shit to work on, but it has nothing to do with you," he said leaning forward now continuing to smoke, "You've proved to me that even without me being here you can handle shit, Preach. I expected you to ride for the crew but you," he pointed. "You truly showed me how solid you are."

I nodded. "I appreciate that. God led me," I said.

There was something else I wanted to ask. Something that had been bothering me for a while. I wasn't sure how he would respond when I asked so I sat up in the chair looking him directly in his face. He'd taught me about looking a man in his eyes when you talk to them, so I was doing just that.

"Are you sick?"

I could see his body still. His body language said a lot. Chevy's head lifted, glancing at me through the smoke. We stared at each other with no words, but the shit was loud. He knew he could no longer dodge any questions I had. He was stuck. For the first fucking time my nigga was stuck. His eyes darkened, and then flickered. I could tell he wanted to speak, but that fear in him held him hostage, so we allowed our eyes to talk to each other instead.

Are you sick, my nigga?

Yes.

I almost felt the wind get knocked out of me. I choked up. My lips betrayed me as they began trembling.

Are you dying?

His eyes squinted.

Yes.

Why didn't you say something, my nigga?

Because it's my burden to bear, not you guys.

I felt tears well in my eyes. I was trying to fight it. Chevy was like my fucking father. I knew it had to be something the night we raced, and he almost hit Harvey. His eyes darkened more as his lips curled up tightly.

Don't say shit.

Got you, my nigga.

Preach, pray in silence, nigga, please.

I nodded, pulling my eyes away. I caught the single tear that slid down the side of my nose as I stood to leave. Chevy stood as well. I wanted to really talk about it, but I was fucked up. I needed to gather my thoughts, and talk to God about it, but I needed to do it alone. I moved toward him, pulling him in for a hug.

"I got you, Chev. I got you," I choked up.

Another tear slid down my face. I pulled away from him dropping my head to wipe my eyes. Chevy said nothing more and neither did I. However, I knew at some point he would have to break the news to everyone. Now everything made sense. My nigga wanted to get to his mother before he died. He had been a savior to us all and there was nothing we could do to save him.

When I got in my car, I drove down the driveway to be out of Chev's sight. I parked my car and broke down. There was no way God was pulling another stunt.

Diamond said he had a surprise for me, and I wasn't sure what it was. I knew he had been trying to get things in order for Gloria's funeral and I was trying to be supportive as much as he allowed me to be. I knew he hadn't resolved whatever issues with Constance, and that alone was probably bothering him. However, he insisted he wanted to go out, so I agreed.

Before I spent time with Diamond my mother had asked all three of us to stop by. When I arrived, I saw my sisters were already there. As soon as I stepped inside the atmosphere was filled with sadness. "What!" I said.

Navi ran to me, "It's Daddy, they found him, he's dead," she sniffled.

My stomach sank. *My Daddy was dead.* I could feel the emotions brewing in me. I didn't know what to think because the reality was, he wasn't a good man. I glanced at Navi who seemed checked out. I could tell it hurt her, but it didn't. It was Zaria who was more torn apart because she didn't know the shit we knew. I rushed over to Zaria embracing her in a hug, "It will be alright Zari," He loved all of us.

My mother sat there zoned out. There was nothing we could say to her in this moment to ease whatever pain she was feeling. I had so many questions, but I wasn't sure I really wanted the answers. Navi stood coming over to me pulling me to the side.

"Did they, do it?" I mumbled.

She pulled her eyes away. "They did!" I squealed.

"Would you shut up. It's not like he was an honest man," she whispered.

"He was still our Daddy!" I snapped.

"Ok. If you're so torn up about it, why aren't you crying? You haven't shed one fucking tear. Listen, I love him I do, but he wasn't right. Let's be there for Ma and Zari," she told me.

Maybe I grieved differently. I couldn't explain why I was emotionless. I'd spend the next few hours with them. When I glanced at my phone, I realized I was thirty minutes late meeting up with Diamond. I left the house trying to call him, but he wouldn't answer. *Shit!*

When I pulled up to the location, he sent me earlier, I rushed inside the building.

"Hi, do you have reservations?" the host asked.

My eyes searched around for Diamond, but I didn't see him. Hell, the place was super fancy, and it didn't seem like his style.

"Ma'am," she said to me.

"Uh sorry, yes, Diamond Blanco?"

She looked down her list of people. "Ah, the special request, follow me." She smiled.

Special request? I followed behind her as she led me to an elevator up to the very top floor. When the elevator opened, she held her hand out for me to get off. As I stepped off there was a candle-lit trail with orange hydrangeas in between each candle. My eyes lit up. At the very far end was a single chair with him sitting in it looking good as fuck. I hadn't even had time to change my sundress I wore. I eased down the walkway until I reached him.

"I thought you were standing me up. I thought you wanted a nigga to chase you," he smiled.

"I'm sorry I had something important going on. Diamond this is beautiful."

"Not more beautiful than you."

He patted his lap. I went to sit but he held his hand out. "Panties off."

"But Diamond," I said looking around.

"It's just you and me, off, now."

I set my purse down coming out of my panties.

"Come to me," he whispered.

I moved closer straddling his lap. "I want to ask you for something. Something I have never asked a woman before. I want something big, something I only want from the person I love, which is you," he said sincerely.

I wrapped my arms around his neck pressing my nose to his. "What?"

"I want you to give me a baby. Can you do that? Can I get you pregnant, on purpose?"

I pulled my head back, "Stop playing."

Diamond hadn't cracked a smile. "I'm serious. I want a family, and I want that with you."

This nigga was serious. Could I see myself with Diamond forever? Did I want little Diamonds running around? I glanced back at him, then smiled.

"Ok. Let's make a baby."

He unbuckled his pants pulling his dick out, "I want you to fuck me right now," he mumbled.

He lifted me up and slid me down so fucking slow my body shook. "Mmm Yana," he moaned sweetly. "Fuck me real good baby," he groaned.

I rolled my hips so slowly I wanted him to feel it every time my pussy circled him. The night air wrapped us in it. I rocked my body to the music playing in my head.

Rock, back and forth. Rock, up, then down.

"Oo baby," I moaned.

Rock, back and forth. Rock, up, then down.

"Yes, baby just like that," he said as he gripped my waist scooting to the end of the chair. He guided my hips as I rocked. We were playing the same tune in our heads. Diamond's tongue captured my neck and licked and sucked all over it.

"My God!" I cried.

Rock, back and forth. Rock, up, then down.

"Pussy so wet, so good, I want that shit to cream up all over me."

Rock, back and forth. Rock, up, then down.

"I love you, Yana" he moaned.

"I love you too,"

"Give me a baby, shit," he moaned louder this time.

My mouth fell open. I placed my forehead to his. He kissed me and I exploded with him right behind me.

Diamond had me wrapped in him and I don't know how our worlds tied together but I was happy they did.

CHAPTER FIFTEEN

DIAMOND

A Little Boy Named Diamond

It was the day for my granny's funeral and my emotions were all over the place. I had spent days going back and forth with Constance about what I wanted for my grandmother, well the lady I knew as my grandmother. It blew my mind that her only concern was the house. Unfortunately, we couldn't find a Will, so the house was going to Constance, and it broke my fucking heart.

We all linked up at my granny's house to be taken to the church. We'd wore all-black suits with orange bow ties, and orange fabric in the breast pockets of our suits. The dark shades on my eyes were to shield myself from the world that my granny had been trying to do for all these years. The limo pulled up and I felt hands to my shoulders.

"You ready my nigga?" Chevy said to me.

I took a deep breath coming down the steps. We entered the limo the entire ride all four of them kept looking at me. I knew they were concerned, but I was just preparing my mind. When we pulled up to the church, my stomach sank. Preach came over to me, "She's still with you, but so are we. We got you," he whispered.

Preach rushed inside to prepare because he chose to give the eulogy. As the service started, we entered. As I came up the aisle, I saw Constance sitting there. She couldn't even sit in the front it was her mother, so she claimed. I then spotted Yana who was in the second row. There were a few more familiar faces I'd remembered from church and the block. My granny had the church packed.

The closer I got to the front and saw my sweet granny peacefully lying there it broke me. My knees buckled. "Man, I can't do this," I turned slightly.

"Come on man," I heard Foe.

I barely made it up the aisle to the front pew sitting directly in front of my granny. I shook my head as the tears trickled constantly. As the service started, and people said some words.

Preach came out and when he spoke with so much conviction, I was done for. Rayana came up to me kneeling before me.

"Diamond, baby, I'm here. I promise," she whispered.

"*Woo,* Lord, help me," I cried.

Preach continued while I tried getting myself together. "Brother Diamond wants to sing a song for Ms. Gloria," Preach said like a true pastor.

I stood easing to the pulpit. Preach leaned in hugging me. "You got this, I love you," he said.

I took the mic and began singing one of my granny's favorite songs.

"*I was born by the river, in a little, Oh and like the river I've been runnin'*"

"Woo, I'm trying y'all."

"*It's been a long, a long time coming, but I know ah-oh- a change gone come.*"

By the end of the service, I was checked out. I gave my granny one last precious kiss to her sweet face before they closed the casket giving her darkness for the rest of her days. All five of us carried the casket out of the church. By the time we went to bury her and got back to her house where I was holding the repass the block was thick. They came out to support me and I felt overwhelmed.

I sat in my granny's room just glancing around at everything. There was a light tap on the door, I turned to look, and it was Constance, she came up to me. "You know I didn't think you loved my mother as much as you portrayed until today. I'm sorry I really am, but I need the keys once this," she pointed around. "Is over."

I nodded. "You know what, you didn't deserve a mother like Gloria and maybe she knew that and that's why she wasn't fucking with you like that!" I snapped. "Those home-cooked meals, the nap time back rubs, the waiting up late, the comfort when you're sick, you didn't deserve any of it. Get the fuck out!" I barked.

She jumped but I didn't care. "Out!"

If it was going to be my last day in this house, I wanted to be alone. Once she left, I stood up, "Fuck!"

Whap!

I hit the wall. I heard something fall in the closet. I opened the door to her bible falling. I picked it up. This wasn't the bible she'd carried before, so I was curious. When I opened it there was an envelope that read: A Little Boy Named Diamond. I opened it.

Once upon a time in a small neighborhood was a young boy named Diamond. He lived in a small house nestled on the far end of the block. Everyday Diamond would wonder off down this block until he stumbled upon a magical house. When Diamond so graciously walked into this house. The smell of good food made his belly rumble. As he explored the inside, he came across someone he didn't know he truly needed, a fairy. His fairy grandmother, who went by the name of Gloria. When he saw her his eyes grew because he'd never seen someone with a smile brighter than hers. His fairy grandmother showed him things. Things his parents never had. So, Diamond found himself traveling to this magical house every day to learn something new. He called it Diamond-Land.

One day Diamond didn't show up to his fairy grandmother's house. So, she went searching for him herself. She used her fairy wings to fly toward the house nestled at the end of the block. When she got there. She noticed something, something that made her sad. She noticed Diamond sitting in the passenger seat of a car with tears streaming down his face. As she looked further that's when she spotted Diamond's mother sleeping, she was in a peaceful sleep that only God could wake her up from. So, the fairy grandmother took Diamond's hand, flying him back to Diamond Land. She comforted him until he went to sleep. When he did, she tried coming up with all kinds of ways to make him happy again, and that's when an idea came to her. She went into the kitchen mixing up a special dust. When she was done, she sprinkled it all over Diamond. That way when he woke, he would know that his fairy grandmother would be his grandmother forever. She waited all night while he slept. When he woke up the next morning, she had a table full of food. When she told Diamond he could stay in Diamond-Land forever, he was so happy. After that, they lived happily ever after.

PS. I love you Chew, if you find this then you have found out the truth. I rescued you from a scary place. Things a kid should never witness. Your mother was running from your father but never made it. I left something for you. I just want you to know I will always love you no matter what happens.

Signed- Your Fairy Grandmother.

By the time I finish reading the letter, it was soaked with my tears. I couldn't believe I didn't remember. I was grateful for her saving my life. I reached into the envelope to pull out the deed to her home and it had my name on it. My granny left me the fucking house, Diamond-Land. A smile eased on my face.

I rushed out of the room so I could show Constance because the bitch really needed to leave now. I moved through the house quickly when I saw her standing there talking to someone. I jogged up to her in the middle of her conversation.

"This house is mine!" I held up the paper.

I could see the guys walking up to me. "Can't be!" she yelled snatching the deed out of my hand.

"And is!" Rayana said. "Now you need to leave."

A few minutes later I could see some niggas coming up the block. It was a bunch of them. A feeling settled in me that wasn't good. Suddenly one for them turned toward us shouting, "Fuck Zoo!"

Rat-a tat -tat -tat. Rat-a -tat- tat- tat.

Screaming and Chaos ensued. My niggas started shooting back.

Bloaw! Blaow! Bloaw! Blaow!

I pushed Rayana to the ground, pulling my gun from behind my back. "Stay here and don't fucking move!" I told Yana.

Bloaw! Blaow! Bloaw! Blaow!

I glanced at Chevy who didn't give a fuck about a bullet as he aimed walking up to them niggas. *Boom! One to head.* One of them dropped.

I aimed and fired again. *Blaow!* Another dropped.

Foe rolled on the ground then jumped up behind of them. *Boom!* Back of the head.

"Where the fuck is Preach?" Chevy yelled.

Preach was on the other side of a car shooting. While Zu shot from the other side.

Bloaw! Blaow!

"Fuck! I've been hit! My nigga I've been hit!" Is all I heard. The few niggas that were left ran off, leaving the street smoky. Some of the people that were left around ran up as we did.

"Fuck!" Chevy yelled.

I could see Yana calling for help. That's when I noticed Constance lying on the ground staring straight up because she had gotten hit by a stray bullet. The piercing screams coming from Harvey brought my attention back as I ran over to see my nigga Foe, lying there bleeding from his side.

To Be continued....

Letter To My Zoo Babies

We've come to another halt as the story continues to unfold. They are growing closer as friends, but also learning to love. The Zoo Boyz is trial and error. As they move along through their journey, they try their best to move forward, but they seem to get pushed ten steps back. However, with the bond they have, happiness doesn't seem too far from their reach.

Preach- stood on business for Navi

Diamond- Lost a love dear to his heart but gained a new one that welcomed him with everything in her.

Zu has been quiet, but I am sure he will step out soon.

Foe – Could karma be catching up to him?

Chevy—the secret is somewhat out, but will he make it to see his mother? Will he allow Zaria to feel whatever void is missing?

This story is one I enjoy and want to continue to elevate on. I know you all are eager for the next book, but remember, once it's over, it's over. I hope you enjoyed Diamond-Land as much as I enjoyed writing it. Now, on to the next!

Until the next one, Zoo Babies!

DIAMOND- LAND

Made in United States
Troutdale, OR
11/25/2024

25287785R00133